"Do you know who I am?"

Laura asked, her voice shaking with emotion.

"I...I remember you from another time you were in here. Are—are you a nurse?"

"No, I'm not part of the hospital staff," she quavered. "Do you know who you are?"

Morgan scowled and closed his eyes. Who *was* he? "I'm sorry...I don't." He studied her. "Where am I? And who are you?"

"I'm Laura Trayhern. Your name is Morgan Trayhern. You're at Bethesda Naval Hospital, in Maryland."

The information was coming too fast. He tried to digest it but didn't succeed. The obvious hurt in Laura's voice tore at him. Her beautiful mouth was pulled into a tight line of suffering that touched some deep, unknown cord within him. He studied her in tense silence. "Are you my sister?"

"I— No, I'm not, Morgan. I'm your wife."

MORGAN'S MERCENARIES:
LOVE AND DANGER:
Four men. Four missions. Each battling
danger to find their way back to love!

Dear Reader,

Silhouette Special Edition welcomes you to a new year filled with romance! Our Celebration 1000! continues in 1996, and where better to begin the new year than with Debbie Macomber's *Just Married*. Marriage and a baby await a mercenary in the latest tale from this bestselling author.

Next we have our HOLIDAY ELOPEMENTS title for the month, Lisa Jackson's *New Year's Daddy,* where a widowed single mom and a single dad benefit from a little matchmaking. Concluding this month is MORGAN'S MERCENARIES: LOVE AND DANGER. Lindsay McKenna brings her newest series to a close with *Morgan's Marriage*.

But wait, there's more—other favorites making an appearance in January include *Cody's Fiancée*, the latest in THE FAMILY WAY series from Gina Ferris Wilkins. And Sherryl Woods's book, *Natural Born Daddy,* is part of her brand-new series called AND BABY MAKES THREE, about the Adams men of Texas. Finally this month, don't miss a wonderful opposites-attract story from Susan Mallery, *The Bodyguard & Ms. Jones*.

Hope this New Year shapes up to be the best year ever! Enjoy this book and all the books to come!

Sincerely,

Tara Gavin
Senior Editor

Please address questions and book requests to:
Silhouette Reader Service
U.S.: 3010 Walden Ave., P.O. Box 1325, Buffalo, NY 14269
Canadian: P.O. Box 609, Fort Erie, Ont. L2A 5X3

LINDSAY McKENNA
MORGAN'S MARRIAGE

Published by Silhouette Books
America's Publisher of Contemporary Romance

To my many other friends whom I enjoy growing with, learning from
and sharing with: Maryann McClusky, Dr. Vickie Menear (Little Sis),
Melissa Assilem, Mary Buckner, Lieutenant-Commander Tim Arkin,
USCG and White House Fellow, Rainbow Joe Bass, D. C. Fontana
(of "Star Trek" fame), Eileen Charbonneau, Susannah Gullo,
Nina Gettler, Bob and Kathy Martin, Glenn Malec (Little Bro) and
Kalina Raphael Rose (my spiritual sister from Australia). I love you all
dearly, and count myself very lucky to have you in my life. Thank you.

 SILHOUETTE BOOKS

ISBN 0-373-24005-8

MORGAN'S MARRIAGE

LINDSAY McKENNA

spent three years serving her country as a meteorologist in the U.S. Navy, so much of her knowledge comes from direct experience. In addition, she spends a great deal of time researching each book, whether it be at the Pentagon or at military bases, extensively interviewing key personnel.

Lindsay is also a pilot. She and her husband of twenty-two years, both avid "rock hounds" and hikers, live in Arizona.

Dear Reader,

In 1983, when I first published *Captive of Fate* with Silhouette Special Edition, I had no idea I'd continue to write for Silhouette Books. Now Special Edition has hit 1000 great romance novels, and I'm thrilled to be a part of a wonderful, continuing tradition.

I have always loved the freedom to write what inspires me. At Silhouette, my interest in the military has been nurtured and supported enthusiastically. With Silhouette's support, I helped to create the subgenre of military romances. It has met with resounding success—thanks to you!

That is why MORGAN'S MERCENARIES: LOVE AND DANGER is an achievement not only for Silhouette Special Edition but for readers who have loved the Trayhern family since LOVE AND GLORY. And everyone, judging from the thousands of letters I've received over the years, fell in love with Morgan Trayhern and Laura Bennett.

Well, after all those years of pleading to see what happened to Morgan, Laura and their family, I have created a four-book series that answers all your questions! This series came about because of *you,* and I hope it gives you as much pleasure reading it as it gave me to write it. So don't think that your heartfelt thoughts and feelings about an author's characters don't count with her and her editors—this is living proof that it does!

I hope you enjoy MORGAN'S MERCENARIES: LOVE AND DANGER.

Warmly,

Lindsay McKenna

Chapter One

It was raining. Or was the sky crying? Laura Trayhern stood rigidly on the steps of the Operations building at Andrews Air Force Base in Washington, D.C., peering anxiously through the gray light of dawn. The Perseus jet bearing her husband, Morgan, trundled slowly toward them. It was February, but instead of snowflakes, cold raindrops fell.

As Laura stood huddled in her tan raincoat, her hands plunged into the deep pockets, a wool muffler encircling her neck, trapping her shoulder-length blond hair, she remembered Morgan telling about that rainy Virginia night seven years ago when he'd been summoned to a general's home. The dying man had sent for him, wanting to reveal the truth about circumstances that had sent Morgan into the clandestine

life of a traitor to his country. It had been the first time
in years he'd stepped back on American soil.

A shiver wound through Laura. If Morgan's situation had been desperate then, it could well be critical
now. How badly injured was he? Less than twelve
hours ago he'd been rescued from a cell at drug-lord
Ramirez's Peruvian jungle fortress by two very brave
and daring operatives. The woman agent, Pilar Mar-
tinez, who had entered the fortress to locate Morgan,
was missing in action. But her partner, Culver Lachlan, a Perseus employee and mercenary, had managed to get Morgan out of that hellhole and onto a
waiting Peruvian army helicopter.

Now Culver was back in the jungle, searching for
his missing partner—and Laura was standing on these
cold concrete steps watching the Lear jet, bearing her
husband, rolling far too slowly toward Operations.
She tried to still her anxiety, but to no avail. Radio silence had been maintained for the entire flight out of
South America, for fear of reprisal attempts by Ramirez. But on board, she knew, was one of the Air
Force's best flight surgeons, Dr. Ann Parsons. Laura
and Morgan knew Ann well, and with the surgeon's
medical knowledge and special expertise working with
men and women traumatized in battle, Morgan was in
the very best of hands.

Still, she had no idea what kind of shape her husband was in. He was alive; the flight team had re-
ported that much by radio once they'd reached U.S.
airspace. Laura squeezed her eyes shut. She felt herself sway. A large hand settled supportively around her
upper arm.

"Laura?"

She lifted her chin and looked up into Jake Randolph's weary, carved features. Since the fateful day that she, Morgan and their son, Jason, had been kidnapped by Ramirez, Jake had taken over the day-to-day running of Perseus for Morgan. And she could see the toll this worldwide marathon of searching out and rescuing them, with the help of three extraordinary merc teams, had taken on him.

"I'm all right," she whispered. But she wasn't, and she knew Jake could see it. Anxiety, rage, worry and sorrow—emotions writhed within her like agitated snakes. Her personal captivity had come at the hands of Garcia, Ramirez's right-hand man, who'd held her prisoner on Nevis Island in the Caribbean. The work of Morgan and his Perseus mercenaries had badly disrupted Ramirez's cocaine trade to the United States over the past year, and the drug lord had decided to get even in the most personal of ways. Luckily, Jason had been relatively well treated and hadn't been physically harmed during his imprisonment. Although emotional consequences were inevitable after such an ordeal, Dr. Parsons had assured her earlier that Jason, due to his age and resilience, would likely be the first to heal. Laura—and Morgan—could take much longer to come to grips with the personal nightmares they'd endured at the hands of Ramirez and Garcia.

"A few more minutes," Jake reassured her, leaving his steadying hand on her arm. "Do you want to wait in the ambulance for him?"

Laura noted the grudging lightening of the sky as drops of rain continued to splash against the gray concrete landing apron—like the heavy tears that threatened to spill from her aching eyes. The ambulance was waiting to take Morgan to the navy hospital in Bethesda, Maryland—one of the best in the nation. Laura didn't know what she would do when she saw Morgan. The wait had been agonizingly long—three months since the kidnapping—and now his freedom was at hand. But what condition was he in? How badly had Ramirez tortured him?

Shivering, she felt Jake's arm go around her shoulders and draw her against him. The man was a giant—like Morgan. Morgan was so tall and proud, towering a good eight inches above her petite frame. For just a moment, Laura allowed herself to lean heavily against Jake. He seemed so stalwart and unyielding, and she felt as if the last of her own strength—the wall she'd erected to survive her desperate ordeal—was rapidly crumbling. Maybe it was the fact that it was all over, and she could let down a little of her careful guard. She had her son back. And now her husband, whom she loved with a fierceness that defied description, was returning to her.

"Laura?"

Opening her eyes, she eased away from Jake. "Y-yes, let's go to the ambulance. I don't want to get in the way when they bring him off the plane."

He smiled slightly, giving her shoulders a reassuring squeeze. "Good thinking. Come on...."

Jake held the black umbrella above her as they stepped off their partially sheltered spot on the wet steps. The rain pounded steadily on the taut umbrella. The temperature was barely above freezing, and as they hurried toward the white ambulance marked with an orange stripe, Laura shivered deeply. Her gaze remained pinned on the approaching Lear jet. *Mor-*

gan. Oh, sweet Lord, how she loved him! Her heart ached, tears stung her eyes and she hung her head. She needed so badly to see him, to assess his condition. Would he be glad to see her? Be able to reach out for her hand—and tell her he loved her?

Her heart began skipping beats as she climbed awkwardly into the ambulance. One of the military attendants who rode up front took her hand, smiled a little and helped her. The bright lights in the rear, where a gurney awaited Morgan, made her wince. The paramedic, a young Air Force lieutenant named Bob Martin, guided her into a seat beside him, and Laura was grateful for the heat blowing from the vehicle's front vents.

She watched anxiously as the jet drew closer. Now she could hear the whine of the engines. Jake stood in the rain, the umbrella folded in his left hand, all his attention on the approaching aircraft.

Laura closed her wet fingers into fists in her lap, starkly aware of all the medical paraphernalia surrounding her. Thank goodness, Dr. Ann Parsons would be accompanying them to Bethesda and would be acting as Morgan's primary doctor. Oh, how Laura ached to see her husband! How many nights had she lain awake, needing his touch and the comforting warmth and bulk of his body next to hers? She even missed those soft snoring sounds he made when he lay on his back and she had to elbow him gently so he'd turn on his side. She longed for so many little things— important things she had never properly appreciated.

"Here they come," Jake said, turning toward her.

The aircraft had stopped, and someone appeared, seemingly out of nowhere, to put chocks beneath the

tires. The engines were cut, the whine rapidly dissi-
pating even as the rain picked up, bouncing off the wet
glare of the concrete. Jake's hair was soaked, the tan
jacket he wore dark with water as he moved toward the
jet's lowering ramp.

Laura's breath became suspended as the two ambulance attendants moved quickly to join him at the
aircraft's opened hatch. A stretcher appeared. Her
heart thudded hard. The still form on it, wrapped
completely in blankets, had to be Morgan. Ann Parsons appeared at the door as the stretcher was lowered to the ground. Laura's hands tightened almost
painfully in her lap.

Lieutenant Martin eased by her, asking her to move
into his unoccupied seat. Her knees weak, Laura got
up, grabbing at anything she could put her trembling
hands on to help her make the move. Light-headed
with anticipation, she heard voices outside the ambulance. The rain was driving hard now, as if the sky
were weeping unabashedly for what Morgan had endured. Instinctively, Laura knew it was a bad sign. Oh,
God, how bad? Did Morgan need emergency surgery? Had he suffered cardiac arrest? she wondered
with terror. She needed so much just to touch his
cheek and let him know that he was finally safe and
that she loved him!

Her eyes widened as the stretcher bearing Morgan
was hoisted aboard the ambulance by two strong men.
Light blue covers swathed his motionless body, pro-
tecting him from the cold and rain. Another atten-
dant handed two IV drips to Lieutenant Martin, who
hung them on hooks above the gurney. Movement at

the opened doors caught her attention: Dr. Ann Parsons.

Laura tore her gaze from the blankets covering Morgan's face as Ann climbed in, her features tight and unreadable. Automatically, Laura's hands went to her chest. The doors slammed shut.

Ann glanced at Laura. "We've got him home," she said a little breathlessly.

The ambulance jerked forward, its lights flashing. At the head of the gurney, Ann quickly pulled the blankets from Morgan's face.

Laura heard someone gasp. Lieutenant Martin worked in tandem with the doctor, very few spoken commands passing between them. The ambulance seemed to move almost drunkenly through the downpour, and Laura's brain leadenly registered that the gasp had come from her, seeing Morgan's face for the first time.

Ann twisted to look at her, then quickly resumed her work, leaning over Morgan, monitoring a blood-pressure cuff around his arm. "He's unconscious, Laura," she said, her voice calm.

Laura fought the panic racing through her as her gaze remained fastened on her husband's slack, grayish face. Shock bolted through her like a lightning strike. This was Morgan? But it couldn't be! This man's face was pathetically thin, his gray skin taut over the sharp bones of his face. Morgan's face was full and strong, not this broken horror. Laura felt terror seep through her skin and muscles to settle into her bones—a coldness leaking to her very soul as she stared at him.

The sounds of the rain pounding on the ambulance roof and Ann's husky orders, the swaying of the vehicle—all ceased to exist in Laura's consciousness. She knew only this man's face—her husband's face—which didn't look familiar at all. Morgan was tall, strong-boned and heavily muscled. This man resembled a prisoner of war starved nearly to death. Morgan had a proud, hawklike nose, but this man's nose was puffy and broken in several places. Her eyes moved to rest on the jet black hair, now peppered with silver at the temples, and those straight, black brows. They, at least, she recognized—remnants of the Morgan she'd laughed with on the night of their seventh wedding anniversary. The night he'd given her a strand of pearls. The night the thugs had broken into their home, shot them with tranquilizer darts and spirited them away to their separate hells.

"Oh, God..." Laura cried softly.

Ann looked up. "He's alive, Laura. Get a hold of yourself."

A lump formed in Laura's throat. Ann's words hit her like icy water—just what she needed to stem the rising tide of hysteria tunneling through her chest. Her fingers curved around her throat as she continued to stare in disbelief at the man on the gurney. Martin changed IVs, and she watched the clear fluid's relentless dripping down the translucent tube into Morgan's arm.

"I-is it him?" she croaked.

Ann handed Martin the blood-pressure cuff and removed the stethoscope from her ears. "Yes, it's Morgan." She reached out, her fingers wrapping firmly around Laura's hand. "He's alive, Laura. Right now, that's what counts."

Nodding jerkily, Laura sat back, still gripping Ann's fingers. The doctor's hands were long and bony, but they were a healer's hands, and Laura was everlastingly grateful that Ann was here with them now. "It doesn't look like him...." she whispered.

"He's been starved," Ann returned quietly. She moved to sit next to Laura. "I've given him a preliminary medical exam, but I'll need to run a lot of tests once we get to the hospital."

"H-has he asked for me?"

Ann's mouth compressed. "No... he's been moving between unconsciousness and semiconsciousness. He's drugged, Laura. His pupils barely respond to light. My guess is he's shot full of cocaine."

Pressing her hand against her mouth, Laura stared down at Morgan—a man she no longer recognized. Tears flooded into her eyes. "How could they do this to him?" Her voice broke with emotion.

Ann put an arm around her and squeezed gently. "That's what these men do. They're animals," she said, her voice vibrating with disgust and anger. "Listen to me, though, Laura. We can give Morgan back his lost weight, help him regain his strength. This is temporary." Worriedly, she assessed her. "What about you? How are you doing?"

"I'm okay."

Ann smiled tiredly and patted her on the shoulder. "Sure you are. Have you been taking the tranquilizers I prescribed?"

Laura shook her head. "I tried, but drugs make me feel out of touch, disconnected. I—I couldn't stand the feeling, so I stopped taking them."

Sighing, Ann nodded. "Damned if you do and damned if you don't."

"Don't be upset with me, Ann. I did try."

The doctor's expression gentled to one of understanding. "I'm not upset with you, Laura. I'm just trying to help you through this awful time. You haven't had a chance to work through your own trauma at all. You had to be there for Jason when he was returned to you...." She looked over at Morgan's deathlike pallor. "Now I'm afraid you'll have an even bigger demand on you."

"I'd rather have my family with me," Laura said in a low, broken voice, "whatever the cost." She had been living on tenterhooks for the past three tortured months, not knowing if Jason was alive; fearing Ramirez had killed Morgan. *Hell.* She'd lived in a hell, with no relief, no moments of reprieve to tend the deep wounds suffered during her own kidnapping.

"So Morgan hasn't come out of it at all? Hasn't asked for me . . . for Jason?"

Ann shook her head. "He's borderline semiconscious at times, Laura. But even then he's so full of cocaine he's not really with us."

"But—he did recognize you, didn't he?"

"No," Ann admitted, "he didn't...."

Laura's stomach began to knot with a terrible foreboding. "Is it normal, when a person's been drugged, not to recognize friends?"

Wearily, Ann pressed her fingers against the bridge of her nose. "Sometimes, in some situations."

Laura looked at this woman who had done so much for all of them. Ann was in her mid-thirties, her dark brown hair glinting with reddish highlights in the ambulance's bright interior. But her skin was taut across the bones of her face, her blue eyes dark and ringed with fatigue. Laura shouldn't be giving her the third degree; the flight surgeon would fight with fierce loyalty through hell itself for Morgan's recovery. It was those very qualities that had led Morgan to actively pursue the Air Force captain for Perseus. Ann's skill not only as a medical doctor but as a psychiatrist specializing in trauma was something he wanted for his employees, who were often caught in life-and-death situations.

No one knew better than Morgan the long-term debilitating effects of trauma. So he'd wooed Captain Parsons away from her prestigious position as one of the Air Force's premier flight surgeons, dealing with field combat and the Post Traumatic Stress Disorder suffered by aviators who had been POWs or had experienced crashes. He'd wanted the best, and Ann had been with Perseus for six of the seven years the company had been in existence. Over the years, Morgan's relationship with Ann had become that of a doting older brother. Ann had grown up without siblings, and Laura knew she considered the Perseus team to be like family.

Reaching out, Laura squeezed her thin hand. "You must be as stressed over Morgan as I am."

Ann returned the grip. "I'm angry, Laura. I'm so angry that, I swear, if I could, I'd put a pistol to Ramirez's head and blow his brains out for what he's done to Morgan." She looked at Morgan and then up at the ambulance ceiling, her voice cracking. "I've seen a lot of PTSD. I'm trained in emergency medicine and trauma. But when I saw Morgan as they took him off that Peruvian helicopter, I cried." She grimaced. "Me, of all people."

"You love him like a brother," Laura reminded her gently.

Ann blinked her eyes and nodded. "Yes, I do." She wiped the tears from her eyes and looked at Laura. "What Ramirez has done to him is unconscionable, Laura. I'll be glad to get him to Bethesda, where we can monitor him. I'll be glad to get this damned cocaine washed out of his system, too. I want to see what's left of Morgan on a mental and emotional level."

Laura fought back her own tears. "Yes...so do I," she whispered.

It was still raining. Laura stood at the window of Bethesda's visitor's lounge, watching the gray pall continue to fall, her arms crossed over her breasts. Time crawled by. When they'd arrived, Morgan had been quickly taken away, never regaining consciousness. That had been many hours ago.

Laura felt more than heard someone approaching. Hoping it was Ann, who was working with the chief of internal medicine on Morgan's many tests, she turned. It was Jake, carrying two cups of black coffee. Searching his exhausted features, she mustered a slight smile as she reached for the proffered white plastic cup.

"Thanks, Jake."

He nodded and eased his bulk against the window frame. "How long is this gonna take?"

Laura sipped the hot coffee. She wrinkled her nose, knowing she'd already drunk too much of the stuff. Still, it seemed somehow soothing and familiar, better than nothing. "I don't know." She sighed.

"I wish to hell Ann could come out and tell us something—anything."

"It's nearly four o'clock." Laura felt the acidic liquid eating at her stomach and set the coffee cup on the table next to the window. The lounge was nearly empty. A young navy petty officer paced on the other side of the room, awaiting the birth of his first child. Life. Life instead of death. Laura's mind was groggy with fatigue and she longed for sleep, but knew it would be impossible.

"I remember," she said softly, turning and looking out the window again, "how Morgan hates the rain. He always said it seemed as if the sky was crying. He never did like tears. When I cried, it always upset him terribly. He never knew what to do, or how to help me." The sky was a dismal gray, though the rain had become soft and sporadic compared to this morning's deluge.

Jake snorted. "Most men have trouble with that. Shah tells me it's good for us to feel a woman's tears, to touch them—that absorbing them into our hands will help us get in touch with our own tears and soften us." He smiled a little. "As you know, my wife is part Sioux. She comes from a culture where people believe in showing feelings."

"Then I wish Morgan had some Indian blood," Laura whispered.

"After seven years of marriage, it still bothers him to see you cry?"

"Yes . . . he's especially sensitive when our children cry. It's almost as if it hurts him physically."

"Well, Morgan has a lot of tears left inside him, Laura. Maybe that's why." Jake sipped the coffee thoughtfully as he gazed out at the gathering dusk. "Night comes on so fast in the winter," he said, more to himself than her. "There's something about this season that's unsettling. I said that to Shah one time, and she laughed. She said winter was the time of turning deep within, of going on an inner spiritual journey. She compared people to seeds strewn over Mother Earth in the fall. We lie there in the elements, rained on, frozen and snowed on. The seed has to pull inward to survive, waiting for a warmer time to come forth." He glanced down at Laura. "Winter is a time to look at who we are—and aren't. The things it's easy to hide from in the many activities of the warmer seasons—our awareness of what's hurting within us, for example—are revealed in this season when we're trapped indoors."

"It gives us time to think, to feel," Laura agreed softly. "I'm glad Shah shared that with you. Winter used to be my favorite time of year."

Jake smiled a little. "You're introspective by nature, Laura. And shy. Shah is, too. I'm more of an extrovert, but Shah has helped me understand that her quiet depth, her need for silence and time alone, isn't wrong. It's necessary to her survival. I like and need people around me. She doesn't. At first, I didn't fully understand that about her, but after we got married, she helped me appreciate introverts in general."

"Eighty percent of the world is made up of extroverts," Laura said wryly. "Morgan's an introvert like me."

"Yes—" Jake sighed "—he is. And maybe that's why he hasn't been able to shed those tears he needs to release." He looked at her worriedly. "What about you? Have you been able to cry? To get out what you're holding on to from your own trauma?"

"Now you're sounding like Ann."

"It's common sense, really," Jake told her in a low voice. "You've lost at least twenty pounds you couldn't afford to lose, Laura. You look like hell warmed over and we're all worried about you."

She reached out and touched his powerful arm. "I'll make it okay, Jake. I've got Morgan back. That's all I need."

He shook his head. "I'm not so sure, Laura. You haven't had a chance to be by yourself and simply heal. You've been on an emotional roller coaster for three months with no down time. Shah's right, I think."

"About what?"

"She told me on the phone a while ago that what you and Morgan need is some quality time together—alone."

"Wouldn't that be wonderful?" It would be, but Laura didn't see how it would be possible.

"It's just a thought," he murmured, sipping the last of his coffee.

Laura turned toward the lounge entrance, and her heart banged once, hard, in her breast. Dr. Parsons, dressed in her white smock, a stethoscope hanging from her neck like a pendant, came through the doors. Anxiously, Laura searched the doctor's worn face.

Automatically, Jake moved to Laura's side and settled an arm around her shoulders, as if to steady her for whatever the doctor had to say.

"Laura, Jake," Ann said in greeting. She put her hands in the smock pockets and focused on Laura.

"How is he?" Laura managed to ask.

"Right now, he's sleeping," she said. "And that's a good sign." She gripped Laura's arm and guided her to one of the vinyl sofas that lined the room. "Come and sit down," she urged gently.

Anxiety rippled through Laura as she sat down opposite Ann. The doctor pushed several strands of dark hair from her eyes.

"The bulk of Morgan's blood tests are back. Physiologically speaking, he's severely malnourished, so we're administering vitamins and minerals via IV." Ann frowned and her voice lowered as she fought to keep the emotion from it. "Ramirez broke three fingers on each of Morgan's hands. The fractures have healed on their own, but two of the six will have to be rebroken and properly set or he'll have trouble with them later. His nose was broken several times, and I'm recommending surgery at a later date to try to undo the damage. His left cheekbone suffered a lateral fracture, but that's healed cleanly. He's lost six teeth, mostly molars—probably from the beatings he took.

"I've got a dentist lined up, and eventually we'll look at bridges to replace the teeth." Ann stopped, took a deep breath, and went on. "Morgan was tortured extensively, Laura. His back is a mass of scars and welts. With antibiotics, all of that should heal pretty much on its own, over time. The scarring will probably be massive, but again, plastic surgery can reduce it."

Ann opened her hands and looked down at them. "There are innumerable cigarette burns on his body."

Laura took in a deep, ragged breath. "My God, Ann—"

"There's more," she warned huskily. "Perhaps the most worrisome is that Morgan so far has no memory—at all. He didn't recognize me. He—he doesn't remember you—"

Laura shot to her feet. "What?"

Jake automatically rose, his hand going to her arm.

Ann looked up at them. "I don't know if it's temporary or permanent, Laura," she admitted. "I've talked to Dr. Williams, the head of psychiatry here, and he says that sometimes, depending on the types of drugs used, the frequency and so on, a person can sustain amnesia...."

Laura felt the hot sting of tears coming to her eyes. "H-he doesn't know me?"

"He doesn't recognize your name," Ann said gently. "Maybe—" she slowly got to her feet "—if he sees you in person, he'll recognize you."

"But he didn't recognize you," she said, her voice terribly off-key.

Ann shrugged. "No... but I'm not his wife, either."

"Morgan's close to you. He loves you like a sister—"

"Laura," Jake cautioned roughly, "let's take this one step at time." He stared at Ann. "Amnesia is usually temporary, isn't it?"

"Yes, but in a case like this, as the drugs slowly leave Morgan's bloodstream, we'll have to see if they've permanently damaged his brain. Once a brain cell is destroyed, it's gone forever. We don't know if the memory portion of his brain has been impaired permanently or not. We're still waiting to do an MRI on him. Right now he's still got too high a level of drugs in his body. In a week or so, we'll do one and see if it shows a decrease in function in that part of the brain."

Laura felt a cold numbness sweeping up from her feet, through her legs and into the center of her body. "I—I thought there would be a lot of physical damage," she babbled, "but I never thought about his brain, his memory.... Oh, my God, what will I do if he doesn't remember his own children? Or me? What—"

"Sit down, Laura," Jake entreated gently, guiding her back to the couch. "Take some deep breaths— you're going pale on us. Do you feel faint?" He gripped both her hands.

Blackness rimmed the edges of her vision. She felt Jake's strong, caring warmth as his huge hands swallowed her small ones. Fear jagged through her, and she gasped and sank back on the couch. Closing her eyes, she tried to steady her ragged breathing. Voices began to swim around her, and she felt Ann's hand on her head, cool palm pressed to her cheek. She felt cold. So cold. Morgan's memory was gone. What if it was permanent? He would have no memory of her as his wife, of the intensity of their love. He wouldn't know his own children.

It was too horrible to contemplate, and Laura felt the icy blackness continuing to sweep upward toward her head. Ann's and Jake's voices became more distant. In moments, she lost touch with physical reality and was swallowed up mercifully, by a womblike darkness that sheltered her from what felt like a near-lethal blow to her emotions. Of all the scenarios she'd played out in her waking hours and in her nightmares over these past terrible months, Laura had never entertained this frightening possibility: Morgan didn't know her. Didn't know any of them. Somewhere, as she spiraled even more deeply into the blackness, she knew that this amnesia wasn't temporary. It was permanent.

Chapter Two

Morgan's world was hazy and filled with nearly unendurable pain. As he drifted in and out of consciousness, torn pieces of voices, faces and experiences shifted in a never-ending kaleidoscope of terror, anxiety and horror. War scenes flashed behind his tightly closed eyes. Sometimes he'd find a moment's rest in a tunnel of light, where he'd stand, looking back toward those horrific scenes.

He felt relief in the white light of the tunnel, a sense of peace that he absorbed like a thirsty sponge and when he walked back toward the twisting, distorted events playing out at the tunnel's end, he felt wrenching pain return on every level of his being. Though he wanted to go toward the opposite end, filled only with the comforting light, something in him said no.

Every once in a while, he'd get a flash of a woman's face—a petite woman with shoulder-length blond hair and the biggest blue eyes he'd ever seen. She looked vaguely familiar, though he didn't know who she was. He did know that when he saw her face amid the clashing pain and suffering, he felt a moment's peace—much like what he experienced in the tunnel of light.

Staring into the depth of this woman's compassionate eyes fed him a sense of serenity and stability that his battered spirit desperately needed. Another woman's face, a younger woman in a naval uniform with short auburn hair, sometimes looked back at him, too. He didn't know her, either, and she didn't bring him the sense of peace the first woman did. And then he'd see a man in his early forties in another uniform—tall, with dark hair. He also saw two very young children, but was at a loss to identify them.

The faces paraded past him, intermixed with the terror and torture of the war scenes that frequently overtook him. He hated it when he gyrated uncontrollably into one of those states because he'd learned to anticipate the pain and anxiety that would come with it—emotions he seemed helpless to fight.

Morgan was exhausted by the cartwheeling sensations and confusing images. He had no idea of time or place. The conviction that he was a prisoner in a nightmarish world that would never end began to wear on him, to the point where he wished he were dead. At least then he could finally rest.

But then the face that gave him solace would return, if only for a moment: the woman with the sunlit hair and sky blue eyes. She made him want to live, to struggle against the scenes that would certainly follow the respite she offered. She made him want to try and hang on, even by bare threads, until her face, her serene presence, would once again fill him with the courage to keep living.

"Ann, you've got to tell me what the MRI results show," Laura quavered. She was standing very still in front of Ann's desk in an office within the Bethesda Naval Hospital. It had been a week, seven horrifying days, since Morgan's return to them. Her hands were damp, knotted tensely in front of her, and she held herself rigidly because if she didn't, she knew her knees would give way.

Dr. Parsons sat behind her large walnut desk scattered with X rays, lab findings and the MRI report. "Please," she entreated gently, "come and sit down."

"I'm tired of waiting for a final answer," Laura whispered, slowly making her way to a chair next to the desk. How many sleepless nights had she endured since arriving at Bethesda? Every night was fragmented with anxiety. Morgan had gone into a coma shortly after arriving at the naval hospital. Ann had said it was due to the high levels of cocaine combined with truth drugs that had been administered in too high a dosage too often during his captivity. They had clashed chemically within his brain and the result had been a war of sorts—with Morgan the casualty, slipping into a coma from the poisonous assault.

With a trembling hand, Laura smoothed a strand of hair away from her eyes. She no longer wore the feminine wool suits that she normally did when out in the world. Wolf Harding, another friend and trusted

Perseus employee, had retrieved some more casual clothes from the house for her earlier in the week. Today she'd donned navy slacks, a long-sleeved white blouse and a brightly woven red-and-gold vest, though she felt anything but colorful. Her deep sense of frustration and loss at this point was beyond tears.

Compressing her full lips, Ann fingered the MRI report. Her voice was oddly low and charged with feeling. "It does show some loss of his permanent memory, Laura."

Pressing her hands against her mouth, Laura stared at the doctor. "No..."

With a grimace, Ann put the report aside. "How much, no one knows."

"So we won't know anything more until Morgan comes out of the coma?" *If* he came out of the coma at all, Laura thought worriedly. She knew that some of Ann's esteemed colleagues felt Morgan would remain in the coma, to become little more than a vegetable. Ann, however, felt differently. Perhaps because she was emotionally attached to the case, to Morgan, she had argued with her psychiatric colleagues that Morgan could rise from the depths he now inhabited. And Laura desperately wanted to believe Ann was right.

Knotting a lacy handkerchief between her fingers, Laura whispered, "What should I do?"

"Keep doing what you're doing," Ann said wearily. "Sit at his bedside, talk to him, read to him, touch him...."

"All right...."

Rubbing her brow tiredly, Ann sat back in the chair and looked up at the ceiling. "I know how awful

Morgan looks to you right now. But you've got to overcome your horror at his condition, Laura, and get in there and fight for him. Do you hear me? When I go into Morgan's room, you're sitting six feet away from him. You don't touch him. Your voice is a monotone when you read to him." Sitting up, Ann clasped her hands on the desk and looked across it with sudden intensity. "I know how much you're hurting. I know how much I'm asking of you, Laura. But if you want Morgan to have a reason to come out of that coma, you've got to put some emotion into what you're doing. Get close to him, hold his hand, talk to him as if he were there and awake, listening to you. You know what I'm saying."

Stung, Laura looked down at her clasped hands. "I feel like it's my fault," she whispered after a moment.

"What? That he slipped into the coma?" Ann got up and came around the desk. She leaned over and gripped Laura's slumped shoulders. "No one is blaming you for your reaction to Morgan or his condition. I know he looks terrible. I want to cry every time I visit him on my rounds. And I'm angry because of what Ramirez has done. I'd like to kill the bastard personally." Ann took a deep breath, steadied her own feelings and said, "It isn't fair to you, Laura. I know that better than most. But I believe that if you give your heart to him, regardless of his present condition, Morgan will respond. I know how much he loves you, how desperately he needs you in his world."

Gripping the handkerchief, Laura bowed her head. "Y-you're right, Ann, as always."

Making an exasperated sound, the doctor gently released Laura's shoulders and crouched down, placing her hands over her friend's. "I'm worried for you, too, Laura. You've got so much riding on your shoulders—again."

Laura gave her a small, sad smile. "This reminds me of the time after I was struck by that car at National Airport. I remember waking up blind in the hospital."

"Then recall those feelings and that time," Ann pleaded. "Remember what you felt like when Morgan came to visit that first time. Remember what you felt like when he held your hands."

Laura lifted her chin and felt a momentary trickle of joy. "He was so strong and capable, Ann. I was terrified at the time. Lost. My sight was gone. I felt out of control. Wh-when Morgan came into my hospital room, he was a stranger. But I homed in on his voice, and when he touched me..." Her voice dropped to a quavering tone. "I felt as if I could make it. Even if I was blind, I knew that with him at my side, supporting me, I could recover." She shrugged. "It was a silly response, looking back. After all, I didn't know him from Adam. Yet there he was. Larger than life, filling my room with his energy, his light, filling me with hope."

"So do the same for him now?"

Laura nodded and squeezed her hands gently. "I understand now, Ann. Thanks..."

It was impossible for Laura to gird herself adequately before entering Morgan's private room. To begin with, she hated hospitals with a passion. As she stepped into the room now, the door quietly closing behind her, she looked over at the bed in the center of all the medical machinery and instruments. At least Morgan wasn't on life-support equipment. Somehow, she had to allow her chaos of emotions to come through no matter what the personal cost to her. Laura forced herself to move forward. She took the chair and moved it next to the bed, within inches of her husband.

Her heart twinged as her gaze moved to his still-swollen face. Morgan was a gaunt shadow of himself. No longer was he larger-than-life, radiating energy much like the summer sun's. Moving almost robotically, she lifted her hand to touch his, but suspended it in midair. All his fingernails had been torn off, and she shivered, unable to imagine the pain he had endured. What kind of monsters would do that to a man?

She sat down and stared at that large, square hand—a hand that had loved her so many times and in so many wonderful ways. Closing her eyes, her fingertips barely an inch from his, Laura allowed those sensations to wash across her, to remind her of their love. Ann was right: she had to allow herself to feel again, regardless of the emotional consequences to herself. Had Morgan abandoned her in her hour of greatest need? No. He'd stuck by her, despite the difficulties presented by her temporary blindness.

Shame wound through Laura as she slowly lifted her lashes and stared down at Morgan's deeply scarred hand. It was the hand of a man who had been forced to walk through hell and had survived it. Now this latest hell could leave him a vegetable. *It isn't fair,* she thought, anger beginning to tinge the depression that had been relentlessly stalking her. Morgan had always fought for the world's underdogs. His company took the dirty little jobs no one in the State Department was willing to take on. He fought for the little people who often didn't have the money, influence or power necessary to rescue their loved ones from some terrifying situation.

A lump formed in her throat as she slid her hand forward until she finally, for the first time, touched Morgan's hand. How cool his skin was! Alarmed, she leaned closer and wrapped her hands around his. It was an automatic response, she supposed. If one of their children, Katherine or Jason, was cold, she'd do the same thing for them. The muscles of Morgan's forearm were weak from lack of use, but the familiar black hair still covered it, and she allowed herself the luxury of closing her eyes as she gently skimmed his arm to reacquaint herself with the feel of him.

How long she'd ached to touch Morgan this way. What had stopped her? Laura knew she was an emotional wreck right now, in so many ways. She was trying to cope. Her therapist, Dr. Pallas Downey, had cautioned her that due to the trauma she'd undergone, plus carrying the responsibility for her children as well as wrestling with Morgan's uncertain condition, she was literally at the end of her rope. Pallas had helped her see the necessity of living life one hour at a time—minute to minute, and nothing more than that.

Laura's mouth softened as she explored Morgan's limp arm. Her fingers glided slowly up and down his skin, and she allowed herself to experience the emotions that went with touching him, even though, for her, to feel meant to hurt—and to remember the seven wonderful years they'd had together. Oh, how happy she'd been! Her gaze moved to Morgan's slack features. His lips were parted and chapped. Leaning over, she touched his full lower lip with a trembling fingertip. She recalled that mouth, how it could twist into a wry smile or a boyish grin of delight—or flatten into a tight line when he was worried. She recalled the feel of his mouth on hers . . . remembering. . . .

Dragging in a ragged breath, Laura stroked Morgan's bearded cheek. He needed a shave. She could do that. Yes, she could do small things for him. She felt the first tentative stirrings of hope since Morgan's return. Maybe, if she did such small, insignificant things as shaving him, holding his hand and reading to him from his favorite books, she could help bring him back—for all of them.

Laura laid Morgan's hand across his blanketed belly. "I'll be right back, darling," she whispered. She would go to the nurse's station, get a razor and shaving cream and some towels. Suddenly, she felt some of the dark depression lift from her weighted shoulders. As she hurried toward the door, she felt hope for the first time since the whole horrifying kidnapping ordeal had begun. And for now that was enough. More than enough.

On the morning of Morgan's fourteenth day at Bethesda, Laura had just finished shaving him and was gently drying the unrelenting line of his jaw with a towel, when she saw his eyelashes flutter. She froze. Had it been her imagination? She had spent the past seven days at his side almost nonstop, silently pleading with him to wake up and find her here at his side, touching him, loving him in small, insignificant ways. Morgan's lashes fluttered again.

A gasp escaped her lips, and she placed the towel on the bedside table next to the bowl of warm water she'd been using.

"Morgan?" she quavered, pressing her hands to his cheeks and framing his face. "Morgan, it's Laura. I'm here. Come to me. Please come to me. I love you, darling. We're all waiting for you to come back to us...."

His lashes fluttered a third time.

Laura's breath jammed in her throat as Morgan's eyelids slowly opened to reveal bloodshot grey ones. He stared up at her, as if not really seeing her. But he must!

"Morgan?" she whispered, disbelief in her tone. "Morgan?"

His mouth closed and then slowly opened. A rasping sound issued from his lips.

Anxiously, Laura captured his hand as he weakly tried to lift it. He was conscious! A thrill shattered through her as she stood, gripping his hand in her own. His light gray eyes remained cloudy and unfocused, but again he tried to speak.

"What is it, Morgan?" She leaned forward, her hair spilling across her shoulder as she pressed her ear close to his lips. "Tell me what you want."

But only rasping, animal-like sounds came from him. No words. Laura's heart was pounding with joy even so. Tears stung her eyes, and she allowed her instincts to take over. When Jason was sick and had a fever, he would awake thirsty and wanting water. Sitting lightly on the edge of the bed, Laura took a glass of water from the table. Dampening a clean washcloth in it, she daubed it gently against his chapped lips. Instantly, he made sucking, drawing sounds.

Trying to still her joy, Laura continued giving Morgan precious drops of water via the cloth. He was so terribly weak! He couldn't so much as lift his hand, and after a few moments, he couldn't move his lips, either. Getting off the bed, she saw his gaze following her. He was still thirsty. Torn between calling Dr. Parsons and remaining at his side, Laura made a decision.

"Here," she whispered, "I'm going to slide my arm under your neck and put the glass to your mouth, Morgan. Then I want you to drink all you want...."

His gaze never left hers. His eyes were bare slits, but Laura could feel him following her movement. Elation made her giddy as she gently slid her arm beneath his neck. Using her own body as a support to raise him just enough to drink from the glass, Laura felt a powerful surge of hope tunnel through her. His head rested wearily against her shoulder and jaw, reminding her more of a newborn baby than a man in control of his own body. But the moment she pressed the edge of the glass to his mouth, he sucked thirstily. As the water flowed to him, he eagerly drank the entire contents. Eight ounces!

Morgan's lashes shuttered closed, as if the effort of drinking had drained what little strength he had, and Laura eased him back down onto the pillow. With a shaking hand, she put the glass aside. Touching his brow, now furrowed and beaded with sweat, she whispered, "Morgan, I'll be right back. I'm going to get Ann for you. Rest, darling. Just rest. I promise, I'll be right back...."

"He's come out of the coma." Ann Parsons couldn't keep the satisfaction out of her voice as she and three other doctors completed their examination of Morgan, who was staring up at them through barely opened eyes. She looked triumphantly over at Laura, who stood tensely to one side, her hands gripped in front of her. A smile tugged at Ann's mouth as she said, "You did it, Laura. All your love and care brought him back. Congratulations."

Shaking internally with fear that the doctors would say Morgan could slip back into the coma, Laura woodenly moved forward. The other three doctors, all men, nodded in agreement and then, offering congratulations, left the room. Laura moved to the bed and gripped Morgan's hand. It was warmer now, and Ann had adjusted the IVs to deliver more fluids, since Morgan was so thirsty. Laura's heart pounded painfully in her breast as she looked down at her husband. How battered and scarred his face was. His old war wound from Vietnam, the scar that carved his flesh from temple to jaw, remained a constant reminder of Morgan's original life-and-death battle, and it had been joined by more recent cuts and bruises.

"Why won't he speak?" Laura wondered aloud as she held his hand and watched him.

"It may take some time," Ann cautioned, replacing the stethoscope around her neck. "Just stay with him, talk to him and be there for him, Laura." She grinned at her with unabashed pride. "You've done one hell of a job! It's got to feel good."

Laura nodded. "I feel like I'm caught in the updrafts and air pockets of a thunderstorm. One minute I'm elated, the next I'm terrorized. I worry that Morgan will slip away from me again."

"I don't think so." The doctor reached over and gripped her patient's shoulder, smiling at him. "Welcome back, Morgan. You've got a whole bunch of people who love you and want you here with them. I'll be back later to check on you." Releasing her grip, she transferred her smile to Laura. "He's all yours. Just keep doing what you're doing. It's working."

The room fell quiet. Laura released a ragged breath as she lowered herself to perch on the edge of the bed, Morgan's hand resting comfortably in her lap. Facing him, she watched his half-opened eyes train cloudily upon her. A slight smile touched her lips as she whispered, "How tired you must be, Morgan." She reached over and slid her fingertips through his black hair, pushing several errant strands aside. "All this commotion. All this excitement." Laura laughed a little. It came out strained, but it made her feel better. "I'm stressed out, too, by all these doctors. What a bunch of eggheads, huh? Three-fourths of them said you wouldn't come out of the coma. Only Ann, the one woman, said you'd come back to me. Thank God she was right."

Laura felt a lump rising in her throat. Sudden tears stung her eyes. "Oh, Morgan, I love you so much...so much it *hurts.*" Leaning over, she placed her mouth gently against his. His cracked, dry ones. She didn't expect him to kiss her in return. She merely wanted somehow to breathe her life, her energy, into him. Kissing Morgan for the first time felt so right. So fulfilling. How she'd ached to kiss him before, but she had been afraid to—until now. She'd wanted to kiss him when he was conscious and could remember her, knowing the love they shared.

Easing her mouth from his, she smiled down into his gray eyes. "I want you to rest, Morgan. I love you. I'll be here for you. I'm going to have my bed moved in here. From now on, I'll sleep nearby. Oh, darling, I'm so glad you're back. We all need you so badly—" Her voice cracked with emotion, and she dashed tears from her eyes.

"Look at me, Morgan. I'm turning into a crybaby. Pallas said it would happen. That I'd have times when the tears would just come, and I should let them. I guess this is one of those times." She squeezed his hand gently, leery of causing him pain. His gray eyes remain fixed on her, and she felt a little vulnerable beneath his unblinking gaze.

"Do you hear me, Morgan? Can you nod your head yes?" She watched for a reaction, but saw none. Concerned, Laura felt a sudden stab of terror. Gently, she ran her fingers up his hand and across his arm. "Morgan? Can you feel me touching you?"

There was no response, only that unsettling, unwavering gaze.

Worriedly, Laura captured one of his hands between hers. "Morgan, I know you're just coming out of the coma. Ann said you might not hear or see everything just yet, that you might drift in and out of consciousness. But, darling, if you hear my voice, please squeeze my hand." Her heart rate soared powerfully as she waited precious moments, aching to feel his fingers move against hers. Morgan's stare never changed. His gray eyes appeared so cloudy. *Oh, please, dear God, let him hear me!*

Just as a scream threatened to unknot in her tightened throat, Laura felt Morgan's fingers curve every so slightly against hers. With a sob of relief, she clutched his hand to her breast. "Oh, thank God," she whispered brokenly. Bowing her head, she pressed small kisses against his injured hand. "I love you, Morgan. I love you so much. I just want you to get well. That's all. I'd sell my soul to the devil himself to see you get up, walk and talk again, darling." Hot tears trickled down her cheeks, dampening not only her fingers, but Morgan's as well.

Gently, Laura pressed his hand against her cheek as she gazed at him through tear-filled eyes. "I love you with my life, Morgan. The children miss you so much. Your family...your friends. Everyone wants you to be well. Please, darling, keep fighting to come back to us. So many people love you...."

Laura saw his eyes change. It wasn't anything obvious, yet because she was not only sensitive, but intuitive to his emotions after seven years of marriage, she felt the subtle shift. For a split second, it seemed as if the cloudiness in his eyes cleared and he was truly with her. Kissing his fingers, she smiled down at him and pressed his hand back against his blanketed chest. "What?" she whispered, leaning down as he began working his mouth as if to speak. "What is it, Morgan? Tell me. I'll hear you...."

Morgan struggled, his lips seeming to have a life of their own as he tried to shape the words ringing through the nearly empty halls of his mind.

Her smile brightened, and Laura grazed his cheek with her hand. "I'm here, darling. Don't fight so hard. Save your strength. You're getting well. You're back with us. I love you so very, very much...." Her hand stilled on his cheek. Morgan struggled more, and she saw it now, clearly, in eyes. They had sharpened in their focus on her, the pupils larger and black—containing some of their old hawklike intensity.

"What?" she whispered, leaning very close to his lips as sounds began to issue forth.

"...Who..."

"Yes?" Laura prompted, excitement in her voice. She'd actually heard the word! "Who?"

Morgan's breath came raggedly as he tried to capture the fragmented sensations and tie them to the correct words. He felt the warmth of her hands on his, felt the warm silk of her hair against his jaw. He *had* to speak! Beads of perspiration formed on his brow as he struggled to corral the words that danced just out of his gyrating mind's reach. Her laughter was spontaneous. When he saw her lift her head, her clear blue eyes shining with happiness, Morgan absorbed her like sunshine.

"Who..." he managed to say at last, his voice rasping hoarsely, "are you?"

Chapter Three

Morgan watched the blond woman's face, glad he'd finally managed to force out the words. His mind was spongy and shorting out. It had taken every last ounce of his diminishing strength to speak. He had so many questions, but was too weak to ask them.

Collapsing against the bed, his head sinking deeply into the pillow after his efforts, he struggled to stay awake, noting the tears that had come to the woman's huge blue eyes. Why? She was beautiful, with a proud quality to the way she held her shoulders and lifted her small chin. Tiny. She was tiny—like a bird.

His lashes drifted shut and he felt himself spiraling back into the darkness. Felt the return of panic. He didn't want to go back to that nightmarish collage of blood, tortured screams and pain. He couldn't stand it anymore. Fighting to remain awake, he felt a warm, trembling touch on his hand. It was *her*. Momentarily, his world stopped spinning as he used every vestige of his dissolving consciousness to home in on her tentative but tender touch. The touch of a healer. A nurse. Maybe she was a nurse, though she wore no uniform.

Nothing made sense. He opened his mouth to protest against his exhaustion and pain. He wanted so desperately to stay awake—to find out who he was, and where he was! In the end, Morgan couldn't win the battle, and sleep claimed him.

The next time he awoke, it was dark outside. He was relieved to again escape the terror that plagued him. His tortured sleep had left him sweaty, and he could feel rivulets making their way down his temples. Weakly he lifted his hand to wipe them away—and realized he was trussed up with tubes and wires like a Christmas turkey. Awkwardly, he lifted his hand to wipe at the sweat. The gesture caused him immediate pain. Confused, he looked at his hand to see why such a small gesture would cause such agony, and was astounded to see that his fingernails were gone, the flesh darkened and ravaged looking as it healed over to create new nails.

What the hell had happened to him? With minute awareness, he began to assess the rest of his body. No matter where he focused, he was either sore and aching or became so if he moved slightly. Had he been in some kind of accident? Opening his eyes wide, he began to absorb his surroundings. A light blue room with stainless steel furniture met his bleary gaze, the venetian blinds open on a night sky.

Sounds began to impinge upon his limited consciousness—muffled voices outside his room. He was in a hospital; he could see that. His brow furrowed. Where was the blond woman? He pictured her thick, golden hair and how it curved to frame her small, pretty features. Then he recalled the hurt in her expression when he'd asked who she was.

His mouth felt cottony, and he longed for a glass of icy cold water. What time was it? Where was he? The questions nagged him as he lay there, needing to talk to someone. The door quietly opened, and his heart gave a powerful leap. The blond woman! A thrill raced through him. Morgan was stymied by his intense response to this stranger. This time, she wore a soft pink, cowl-necked angora sweater and black slacks. The pale shade of the sweater highlighted her wan features, and Morgan saw the telltale purple circles beneath her glorious eyes. He sensed an incredible sadness around the woman as she closed the door behind her.

When she turned and saw that he was awake, she became rooted to the spot. He felt the intensity of her gaze, saw hope flare in those wonderful eyes of hers that couldn't hide her feelings. Morgan felt like an intruder as he clung to that gaze. She wore her vulnerability on her sleeve, and he could not only see her emotions register but feel them, too. It was a startling discovery, almost as if he were a mind reader privy to this woman's inner world. Momentarily embarrassed, he tore his gaze from hers.

"Water..." he rasped.

"What?"

Morgan made the effort to look at her again. She moved almost robotically toward him, anxiety plain on her fine features. Working to make his lips move again, he whispered, "Water...please..."

She moved jerkily. "Water. Yes...hold on a moment." She reached for the plastic container and poured him a glass.

Morgan didn't know which he wanted more—her touch or the water. He remembered her tender caress from before. How long ago had that been? Time was meaningless to him. He tried to sit up, but his efforts were short-lived. As she came to his bedside, she leaned over him, and he inhaled deeply, savoring the fragrance of camellia. When she slid her arm beneath his sweaty neck, Morgan groaned. It was a groan of pleasure, but she must not have realized it, because she stopped and stiffened.

"It's...okay...." he assured her gruffly, struggling to rise enough to drink.

"Take it easy," she urged a little breathlessly, continuing to slide her arm around his neck and lift him enough to press the rim of the glass to his lips.

The water was heavenly. He slurped it down like a man too long in the desert. Wildly aware of her soft, strong body supporting his, Morgan was content to rest his head against her. This woman was soft, yet strong. She gave him three glasses of water before his thirst was sated. As she eased him back down on the bed and nervously fluffed the pillow around his head, he studied her from barely opened eyes.

"You...smell good.... Better than this damned hospital...."

She stopped fluffing his pillow and stared down at him. "It's camellia. Your favorite perfume."

Morgan frowned. "Mine?" His voice was rough from disuse, and words wouldn't flow together like he wanted them to. He saw pain in her eyes, and her soft lips compressed.

"Do you know who I am?" she asked, her voice shaking with emotion.

Morgan watched her steel herself against his answer. Her fingers rested tentatively against the edge of his bed, and she held herself almost rigid, waiting for him to speak. "I...no, I don't know you. I... remember you from another time when you were in here, though. A-are you a nurse?"

"No, I'm not part of the hospital staff," she quavered. "Do you know who you are?"

Morgan scowled and closed his eyes. Who *was* he? Opening his lashes, he stared up at her. "You called me Morgan. I guess I'm Morgan."

"D-do you know your last name?"

He rolled his head slowly from side to side. "I'm sorry...I don't. And I don't know where I am. Or how I got here." He studied her. "Where am I? And who are you?"

"I'm Laura Trayhern. You're Morgan Trayhern. You're at Bethesda Naval Hospital, in Maryland."

The information was coming too fast. He tried to digest it but didn't succeed. The obvious hurt in Laura's voice tore at him. He saw tears form in her eyes—saw her battling to keep them from spilling down her pale cheeks. Her beautiful mouth was pulled into a tight line of suffering that touched some deep, unknown chord within him.

His name was Morgan Trayhern. She was Laura Trayhern. He studied her in the tense silence. "Are you my sister?"

"I—no, I'm not, Morgan. I'm your wife...."

He stared at her, shocked. He saw such anguish in her eyes, and he longed to ease that pain. But how? Nervously, she clasped her hands in front of her and bowed her head. Why couldn't he remember such an important thing? Stunned by the information and feeling her pain, he muttered, "How long have we been—married?"

Laura lifted her head, fighting the urge to shriek out her grief. She saw the genuine confusion in Morgan's features. "Seven years, Morgan." She watched the information strike him as surely as if she'd hit him with her fist. It was shock, not joy, that registered in his eyes. A sob lodged in her throat, and she swallowed hard. Right now, Morgan didn't need her tears. He needed answers. Maybe Dr. Parsons was right: they should give Morgan the information as he asked for it. Perhaps it would stimulate memories—if any were left undestroyed by the drugs. Oh, what if Morgan *never* remembered who she was or what they'd shared?

Laura felt such a gutting pain surge through her that for a moment she couldn't breathe. Three days ago, Morgan had awakened from his coma and haltingly asked who she was. Now he was fully conscious and able to speak coherently, and she should be grateful—but she was living in a nightmare where her carefully knit strands of hope were unraveling before her eyes. He didn't know her. He didn't remember their love. Or their marriage.

Through a sheer effort of will, she forced herself to put her own suffering aside and focus on Morgan. He was extremely pale, but his strength had improved noticeably, and his gray eyes, once so cloudy, held more of their old sharpness. Laura knew he was still emerging from the drugged state, but at least he was functioning, and for that she had to be grateful. She ached to reach over, caress his shaven features, kiss him and tell him of her great love for him. But she could tell by his stymied expression that he wouldn't accept her gesture. He was staring at her with bewilderment—as if she were a total stranger.

"How did I get here?" he demanded, his voice stronger.

Laura brought over a chair and sat down. Ann had told her to answer whatever questions Morgan had—thoroughly, but slowly, so that the information could be absorbed. "You own Perseus, Morgan. It's a company that hires mercenaries to undertake jobs around the world. Many times you've worked with our government—or with another country's government—to help people who are being held prisoner or in some other kind of danger."

Laura saw his black eyebrows knit as he digested the information, and prayed that something—anything—she told him would spark a latent memory within him. She needed a sign that some remnant of his former life—of her and their children—remained. Her palms were damp as she continued. "You've owned the company for seven years. Three months ago, you and I, and our son, Jason, were kidnapped by a drug lord named Ramirez." Her voice faltered and became strained. "Jake Randolph, one of your employees, took up the reins of Perseus in your absence. With the help of the government, he located us, one by one. I was the first to be rescued, then Jason, and now you."

Morgan stared disbelievingly at her. "A-are you making this up?"

Laura sat very still. Anger lapped at the taut edge of her patience. "How could I be?" Her voice echoed around the room—strident, pain-filled and off-key. Nervously, she touched her brow. "I-I'm sorry, Morgan. No, I'm not making any of this up. I just want you to remember so badly... but you don't... and—"

"It sounds like a James Bond movie," he muttered. Looking away, he stared at the dark void of the window. His conscience pricked him. He heard the hurt in Laura's voice, felt her pain as if it was his own, but dammit, he was hurting too much himself. It took every ounce of his strength to concentrate on her words—and the strange ideas she presented—instead of giving in to the aches of his physical body.

Laura reached out, her fingers curving around his arm. At least he remembered James Bond. That was good. But at what age had he seen those movies? Had his memory been wiped out back to that time? Or was this a meaningless fragment? Instantly, she felt Morgan react, his muscles tightening beneath her fingertips. She released him, and he rolled his head toward her, his eyes dark and angry. Stung by his reaction, she swallowed against the lump in her throat that refused to go away. "You've suffered so much, Morgan," she began in an unsteady voice. "We all have."

"I don't remember anything," he rasped. "I wish I did, but I don't. Hell, if you hadn't told me my name, I wouldn't even know that much."

Standing up despite her weakened knees, Laura whispered, "I know... and it's all right, Morgan. Dr. Parsons said your memory would be influenced by the drugs you were given."

"What drugs?"

Laura took in a deep breath and said in a low voice, "Ramirez wanted to get even with you for damaging his Peruvian cocaine empire. Over the years, you sent many missions to stem the flow of cocaine traffic to the eastern United States. It worked—too well. Ramirez kidnapped the three of us to stop you. To...get even, I guess." Wearily, she touched her brow, a headache lapping at her temples. It was nearly three in the morning, and something had awakened her out of badly needed sleep down in the nurse's quarters, where she'd been spending the nights since Morgan had become conscious and failed to recognize her.

She'd quickly abandoned the idea of bringing a bed into his room. What was the use? He didn't know her from Adam. Laura couldn't stand the thought of him looking at her the way he was now—as if she were some bug under a microscope rather than his devoted wife.

Morgan watched Laura in the stilted silence. Suddenly, he was very tired. And he felt old. Very old. No question, Laura was hurting. She was his wife—of seven years. So why the hell couldn't he remember? He focused on his heart, searching for emotion, but he found no lingering tendrils of love. Frustration ate at him, and his mind whirled with the strange information she'd imparted. He had no reason to disbelieve her. Her face was that of an innocent angel. She seemed incapable of lying.

"Listen," Laura whispered as she came back to his bedside, careful not to touch him this time, "you need to sleep, Morgan. You're still recovering, and it's three in the morning. Dr. Parsons will be here at eight o'clock to see you. You've known her a long time." She managed a partial smile. "I'm glad you're out of the coma. I'm glad you're back with us."

Closing his eyes, Morgan felt bitterness leaking through him. Who was "us"? He had a family. He had a son named Jason. Why the hell couldn't he recall that information—or at least feel some emotion? He felt her tug gently at the blanket and sheets, tucking them more snugly around him. Then she left, as quietly as she'd come.

Morgan was not only wide awake at eight, he could hardly wait for this Dr. Parsons to come through the door. He had a lot more questions to ask, and he wanted answers. Despite all the tubes, he'd managed to drag himself into a semi-upright position. Finally the door opened, and a tall dark-haired woman in her thirties entered. Morgan waited to recognize her, but sensed nothing familiar. A name badge on her white coat read Parsons. She carried a clipboard, a stethoscope hung around her neck and a smile of genuine welcome lit up her face.

"Morgan. It's good to see you awake and so alert."

He scowled. The doctor laid the clipboard on the table and reached out her hand. Weakly, he raised his. Her grip was warm and firm.

"Hmm, you're stronger than I thought you might be," she murmured, her voice pleased as she looked intently into his eyes. Releasing his hand, she smiled. "How are you feeling?"

"I'm thirsty as hell, Doctor, and I need to get all these damned tubes out of me."

Laughing, Ann placed the stethoscope in her ears and listened to his heart and lungs. "You're an amazing man, Morgan. But you always were."

Morgan lay impatiently as she examined him thoroughly, from his hands to his back, which smarted like hell itself, to the rest of his body. "I don't know you," he said abruptly when she'd finally stepped back. "Laura said I would know you, but I don't."

Ann sobered and reached forward to pull the covers up over him. "She told you about the drugs Ramirez gave you?"

"Yes." He felt highly impatient. Angry. "Dammit, Doctor, my head is *empty*. I don't remember anything. When the hell is that going to change?"

"I don't know, Morgan. I wish I had an answer for you, but I don't. Damage has occurred to the memory-storage part of your brain because of the cocaine and other drugs Ramirez used on you."

"Ramirez..."

She sat on the edge of the bed, facing him. "Do you remember him?"

"Hell, no! But if I did, I'd like to kill the son of a bitch for erasing my memory."

"He tortured you. Did Laura cover that with you?"

Breathing hard, Morgan shook his head. "No."

Pursing her lips, she said, "I see."

"Well, I'm glad as hell someone does." He glared up at her. "This woman, Laura..."

"What about her?"

"She says she's my wife." He made a frustrated sound and looked away from the doctor's somber features. "If she is, why the hell can't I feel anything for her?"

"You feel nothing, Morgan?"

"Nothing," he said flatly. "And I feel bad, because I can see it hurts her." Working his mouth, he muttered, "I don't want to see her hurt...but dammit, I can't force myself to feel something that isn't there!"

"Of course you can't," Ann said soothingly as she eased off the bed. "First things first, Morgan. I'm going to have a nurse come in and remove these IVs. I think you're ready to try solid food. Later, we'll send some orderlies in to get you on your feet and start working those leg muscles. Right now, you're weak as a newborn lamb."

He tried to steady his breathing. "Isn't there someone I'd remember?"

"You don't remember me at all?" she asked as she picked up her clipboard.

"No."

"This afternoon," she said, "I'm going to ask several of your friends to drop by. They won't stay long, just long enough to see if it jogs something in your memory."

He scowled. "And if nothing jogs? What then?"

"We'll take this one day at a time, Morgan. Sometimes, as the drugs wash out of a person's system—which can take weeks—a memory might return. It might be something small and insignificant, but it would be a start to opening the door on all of your past.''

Morgan looked down, feeling completely alone. ''Do you know what it's like to sit here without a past, Doctor? My memory is a big blank. I've got nothing!''

Ann reached out and gently touched his gowned shoulder. ''Take it easy, Morgan. I know how upsetting this is. But don't push yourself so hard—don't try to force the memories.'' She pointed to the television affixed to the wall opposite his bed. ''I suggest watching some television, and I'll have a nurse bring you some newspapers and magazines. Anything might trigger a memory.''

Bitterly, he looked around the sterile room. ''I hate hospitals.''

A smile turned up the corners of Ann's serious mouth. ''Well,'' she drawled, ''at least that sounds like the old Morgan speaking.''

''What?''

She grinned a little. ''You've always hated hospitals—and with good reason.''

''Tell me why.''

''No,'' Ann said lightly, ''my gut feeling is you'll remember on your own. It's just a good sign to me that you might know more than you think you do. Your responses are those of the Morgan I knew before this ordeal. Trust your gut feelings, your inner knowing, Morgan. That will help open that door to the past, too.''

''Feeling? Knowing?'' He growled the words like a snarling dog. ''I'm a man, Doctor. I don't work off feeling and knowing. I go by what I can see, hear, taste or smell."

She chuckled indulgently and patted his arm. "Yup, you're the same old Morgan. Welcome home, my friend. It's good to have you back. I'll send in a nurse shortly to untruss you."

Morgan watched her walk to the door and open it. "Wait."

Ann turned expectedly. "Yes?"

"What—what about Laura?"

"You tell me."

He glared at her. "I don't want to keep hurting her."

Shrugging, Ann murmured, "Neither of you has that choice right now. She loves you. You're her husband."

"But I don't remember her!" he exclaimed, frustrated. "I can't pretend with her, Doctor."

"No, and you shouldn't, Morgan."

"Then what the hell am I to do?"

"Be patient. I know it's not one of your finer attributes. You've never been particularly patient—except with Laura and your children. But you're going to have to try."

"When will I see her?"

"She's sleeping right now. I gave her a sedative that will knock her out for at least eight hours."

Morgan stared down at the light blue bedspread. "She's hurting badly over all this. I can feel it."

Ann shut the door and walked back to his bed, holding her clipboard in front of her. "Morgan, she's very fragile," she warned quietly. "Did she tell you anything of her own kidnapping ordeal?"

"No," he growled impatiently, "only that she and Jason, my son, were kidnapped along with me."

"That's all?"

"That's all."

Ann looked up at the window and then back at him. Her voice was gentle. "She's suffering as much as you, Morgan, for a lot of reasons that I'm going to allow her to tell you when she feels the time is right. Laura is one of the most valiant women I've ever run across in my life, and I've seen a few heroes in my lifetime, believe me. She's been a main support for you, Perseus and everyone connected with these horrible events."

"She's vulnerable," he observed tiredly. "I can feel it around her and see it in her face."

"Yes," Ann agreed.

"So I'm not aiding things by not remembering. Hell," he rasped, "I feel no connection with her! She's a stranger to me, Doctor." His voice cracked with concern. "I can see she needs help but I don't know how to help her. I mean, I feel for her, for whatever she's going through, but I can't make that personal connection that a husband and wife would have. I don't know what the hell to do—" His voice cracked.

Ann nodded. "I know," she whispered. "It's a painful situation for everyone, and it's not going to go away, Morgan. As a psychiatrist, my response is that you should spend as much time with Laura as you can. It will better your chances of remembering. She was close to you, Morgan, more than anyone else in your life. You trusted her. You didn't let people get very close to you because of—ah—your past. But Laura was able to get beyond your defenses. She knows you best, Morgan. That's why it's so important you allow her to remain in your life.''

An acidic taste stung his mouth as he avoided the doctor's searching look. "All she does is make me feel more pain. I've got enough of my own. I don't want to feel hers, too."

Sighing, Ann nodded. "Give yourself some time, Morgan. Laura has a lot she's dealing with right now. She can no more hide her pain than you can yours. It's a raw situation with no easy answers."

Leaning back on the pillows, exhausted, Morgan shut his eyes. "I'm so damned angry and upset," he rasped unsteadily. "I want to cry for myself . . . for her. . . ."

"That's a good sign, Morgan."

His eyes snapped open and he looked at her. "What is?"

"The fact that you want to cry for both of you. Stay with your feelings. Stay with Laura. She helped you once. I know she can help you again. . . ."

Chapter Four

Morgan moved restlessly around the hospital room. It had been two weeks since he'd come out of the coma, and he was bored to death. Weak February sunshine filtered between the slats of the venetian blinds. Outside, at least a foot of snow covered the ground. How he longed to be out there! Holding the blinds apart with his healing fingers, he wondered if the *real* Morgan Trayhern also loved the outdoors.

He frowned, and his mind swung back to Laura. She was his wife in name only. No matter what she said or what pictures she showed him of his family, he couldn't find that answering connection within him. He eased his fingers from the blinds and turned around. His level of confusion was almost too much to cope with. Over the weeks, different people—friends and employees from his past, he was told—had visited him. He recognized none of their faces or stories. Not a damn one.

Morgan sighed and ran his fingers through his short black hair sprinkled with silver. Turning, he walked slowly back to the unmade bed. Newspapers, magazines and videos were scattered all over the place. In one way, he supposed, he'd caught up with the world at large. Jake Randolph was continuing to run Perseus for him—and Morgan couldn't imagine trying to run it himself. The Morgan Trayhern they knew evidently had a commanding grasp of military knowledge, but he certainly didn't.

His scowl deepened. On the dresser sat a photograph of his younger sister, Alyssa Cantrell, and her husband, Clay. Another photo showed his brother, Noah, Noah's wife, Kit, and their children. A third photo showed his smiling parents in front of their Clearwater, Florida, home. He recognized none of them.

The door opened.

In relief, Morgan looked up. Who would it be this time? Dr. Parsons had scheduled visitors for him on a daily basis. He got a briefing from Jake at eight o'clock every morning, though he felt foolish that the names, the teams and their objectives meant nothing to him at all.

Jake poked his head around the corner. "Good morning, Morgan," he said in greeting.

"I suppose," Morgan growled. "Come in." Jake was wearing a red flannel shirt and Levi's. For a man running a multimillion-dollar company, he certainly didn't look the part. He looked more like a soldier than an executive. Morgan wondered how he himself had dressed when he'd run Perseus, but decided not to ask. Jake had his briefcase in hand, and he hoisted it up on the bed between them.

"We're switching tactics today," Jake said without preamble as he opened it.

Morgan halted in his tracks. "Oh?"

"Yeah, you and Laura are going deep undercover for a while." Jake eyed him, then handed over a piece of paper. "We picked up a satcom from Peru late yesterday."

Morgan read it. "It's from Guillermo Garcia."

Jake sighed. "That's right, Ramirez's right-hand man. Ramirez may be dead, but Garcia has wasted no time in taking over his cocaine empire." Stabbing one finger at the paper, Jake said worriedly, "He's sending out several professional hit men to get rid of you, Laura and your family."

Morgan studied the paper intently. His mouth hardened. "I wish like hell I could remember, Jake. Garcia's name means nothing to me."

"Doesn't matter," Jake said abruptly. He picked up some photos and handed them to him. "We had a conference this morning, and we feel it best to do two things. This has Dr. Parsons's approval, by the way."

Morgan took the photos. "What's been decided?" One of the pictures was of a ranch in dry, desertlike surroundings. Another showed a small log cabin near a stream lined with pines and white-barked trees.

"Your children, Jason and Katherine, are going with Susannah and Sean Killian. They'll be deep in the woods of Kentucky at a location only I will know about. You and Laura will go into hiding at the Donovan Ranch, in a canyon in central Arizona. You knew

Robert Donovan. In fact, his son, Randy, was in your company when it was overrun by the Vietcong. Mr. Donovan and his wife recently died in an auto accident, but his daughters are running the ranch, and they said you and Laura were welcome.''

His mouth quirking, Morgan looked up. "Laura is going with me?"

Jake gave him a flat stare. "She's your wife."

Struggling to know how to react, Morgan said nothing.

Exasperated, Jake growled, "She's on Garcia's hit list, too. The son of a bitch is going after all four of you this time. And he's taking no prisoners, Morgan. I don't think you want Laura left behind as a target."

"Of course not," Morgan snapped irritably.

"Look," Jake said, suddenly weary, "I know you're not remembering anything. I can't imagine me not knowing my wife, Shah. I don't know what the hell I'd do, either, but I know if we were under attack, I'd still want her with me."

Angrily, Morgan turned and walked back to the window. "My marriage isn't any of your business."

"I saw the look on your face," Jake warned, coming over to the window and joining him. He settled his large hands on his narrow hips as he studied Morgan. "Two other people will go with you," he said slowly. "They'll stay at the main ranch house, about fifteen miles from this small cabin on Oak Creek." Jake jabbed a big finger toward the pictures Morgan still held. "Dr. Parsons is going, for obvious reasons. An Army Special Forces officer, Major Mike Houston, who's had a lot of years in Peru chasing Ramirez and his likes, will accompany you. He's your professional insurance against an attack by these hit men Garcia's sending stateside.''

Morgan inhaled a deep breath, fighting the anger and frustration roiling within him. ''Dammit, Jake, I *wish* I could remember!''

''Like Ann said, stop trying to remember specifics. Trust your feelings. They'll eventually open those doors.''

Glaring at him, Morgan snarled, ''Feelings? The only thing I feel is mountain-sized frustration. How do you think I feel when Laura comes to visit and I can read every unhappy emotion on her face?''

''She's wounded, too,'' Jake reminded him slowly. ''Has she talked to you about her capture by Garcia?''

''Hell, no!''

''Have you asked?''

''No...''

''I think,'' Jake growled, ''you're feeling real sorry for yourself, Morgan, for your plight. Maybe I would, too. But you're being pretty ungrateful about all the help you're getting, if you ask me.''

Morgan turned and held Jake's dark stare. ''Just what the hell is that supposed to mean?''

''Take the focus off yourself, Morgan. Laura needs you. You're the only one who can help her,'' Jake said huskily. ''I don't care to hear your lament about not remembering her as your wife. Dammit, you have to begin treating her like a *human being*—somebody who cares enough to come daily to this room to see you— rather than as some inconvenient fixture.''

His nostrils flaring, Morgan knotted his hands into fists. He took in Jake's implacable expression, the slashed set of his mouth as he held Morgan's gaze. "I suppose she's been running and crying to you."

Jake clenched his teeth. "Morgan, you're being pigheaded, but then, you were always that way, even before the amnesia. No, Laura hasn't run to me or anyone else. That's the problem—she's bottled everything up. Dr. Parsons is really worried about her. Laura has taken too much for too long and has nowhere to safely dump her feelings. You sure as hell haven't been much help."

"She can talk to me if she wants to," Morgan snapped, moving away from the window. Who the hell did Randolph think he was?

Jake followed closely. "Morgan, maybe this quiet little cabin in a canyon is exactly what both of you need."

Halting at the bed, Morgan shot a look over his shoulder. "I don't know what you're talking about."

"The old Morgan I know always got back in touch with nature to unwind. The place you're going was a favorite of yours when you were a young officer in the Marine Corps. It's isolated, with a lot of wildlife and trout fishing—no people except the ranch hands and owners. Laura needs a break from all of this." Jake took the photo of the log cabin and studied it. "Right now, we're more worried about her deteriorating condition than about you. You're going to live. You've survived the worst, physically speaking."

"All right," Morgan rasped, "I'll go. I'll try to help Laura, but there's no guarantee."

Jake dropped the photo on the bed and smiled a little. "I have a hunch that this is exactly what you both need. Mike Houston will be around, but you won't see him unless he wants you to. He's a professional soldier, and he'll make sure Garcia's hit men don't get close enough to take a shot at you. Dr. Parsons is coming along more because of Laura's emotional instability than for your health needs, although Laura doesn't know that. I'd appreciate it if you wouldn't say anything to her.''

"I'm not the kind of person to deliberately hurt someone,'' Morgan snapped.

A rueful smile pulled at Jake's mouth. "Morgan, you're a contrary bastard by nature, but I understand why. The only place in your life where you weren't like that was with Laura and your kids. With them, you finally exposed your soft underbelly, and that was the only time you did. Take this time at the cabin and let that side of you surface with Laura. You trusted her more than anyone else in your life. . . .''

"It's beautiful,'' Laura breathed. She stood beside a muddied Jeep driven by Rachel Donovan, the oldest of the three daughters now running the Donovan cattle ranch. In front of them, at the end of the muddy road, stood a log cabin. It wasn't large, but it was a stone's throw from the rushing waters of Oak Creek.

"We think you'll love it here,'' Rachel said cheerily. "It's been a favorite hideaway for our friends and family over the years.''

Laura looked hopefully up at Morgan, dressed in a white, long-sleeved shirt and Levi's. His face had lost a little of its tension as he looked at the cabin. Their flight to Luke Air Force Base near Phoenix, had been long but uneventful, and for that she was grateful. In her peripheral vision, she saw Rachel pick up their luggage. Days earlier, Major Houston and Dr. Parsons had flown out and were already staying at the main ranch. Laura had met Mike and liked him immensely. She knew he had been instrumental in rescuing Morgan from Ramirez in Peru.

"What do you think?" Laura asked Morgan.

"It's nice," he grunted. Moving forward, he reached to help Rachel with the bags. The ground was covered with pine needles, but the soil was clay, and it stubbornly stuck to his shoes. Rachel had warned them that cowboy boots would be the uniform of the day. Above them, the Arizona sun shone brightly. It was the end of February, and the temperature was already in the high fifties, with no snow in sight. The cabin was located about ten miles north of the small town of Sedona in a huge canyon filled with pine trees and white-barked sycamores. The walls of the canyon, Rachel had told them as she made the drive up the narrow road to the cabin, consisted of red and white sedimentary sandstone, laid down millions of years ago and layered with black basalt—the remains of lava from the volcanic activity that had been a big part of the region's prehistoric past.

Picking up their luggage, Morgan strode into the cabin. It was small—only four rooms. Panic surged within him as he noted that there was only one bedroom. Rachel smiled and pushed some of her reddish brown hair away from her face after hefting two suitcases onto one of the room's twin beds.

"We use this cabin during branding season," she said, sweeping her hand around the room. "The twin beds are all we have."

Morgan stared at them. The room was small, the two beds covered with light pink chenille spreads. The windows were open to allow the clean, pine-fragrant air to circulate. "It'll be fine, Rachel."

"Good," she said with relief. "I'm going to give Laura a quick tour of the kitchen facilities."

Morgan stood alone in the quiet bedroom. At least they'd have separate beds. Still, he was uncomfortable with the idea of Laura being so close to him at night, though he wasn't sure why. Since the day he'd come out of the coma, he'd watched her gradually retreat from him in a number of ways. Could he blame her? He certainly wasn't reaching out to touch her or show her any kind of intimacy a husband might share with his wife. But how could he? Still, her increasing silence spoke louder than words. Maybe Jake was right, and he should pay more attention to his feelings. It was as if an invisible cord was strung between him and Laura—one composed of instinctive responses that he fought daily to ignore.

Turning slowly around, Morgan opened his suitcase and pulled open one of the dresser drawers. Laura kept up a smiling exterior and was excellent at small talk, but he could feel her hiding a lot deep within her. He heard the sudden chatter of chickadees outside the window, joined by the high squeak of a flicker. Going to the screened window, he spotted the rust red underwings of the flicker on a branch of a pine not far from the cabin. Funny, he recognized those sounds, and he'd known automatically what kind of bird made them. Maybe, he ruminated, returning to his unpacking, he shouldn't give up hope yet.

When he'd finished putting his clothes away, he opened Laura's suitcases. His hands stilled as he saw several photos in a plastic bag lying on top of her clothes. Over the weeks, Laura had brought several photos to him in hopes of jogging his memory. These, he knew, were framed photos of his children, and one of their entire family. Fingering them, Morgan felt an odd emotion flow through him—the first of its kind. Holding the photos, he savored the odd feeling.

"Morgan?"

He lifted his head at the sound of Laura's voice. She stood hesitantly in the doorway. Her blond hair had been swept back, captured into a girlish ponytail with tendrils at her temples that emphasized her very readable blue eyes. Morgan noticed she'd changed from the dark green silk shirtdress she'd traveled in, into a bright pink, long-sleeved blouse and jeans. His lower body tightened in appreciation. For a woman who'd had two children, she still had a body that could make any man look twice.

"Yes?" His voice came out off-key, and he saw her eyes become shadowed as she saw him bending over her suitcase, photos in hand. Did she think he was snooping without permission?

She smiled hesitantly and moved to the end of the bed. "I see you found the family photos."

"Yeah," he grunted, handing them to her. As his fingers touched hers briefly in the exchange, that same feeling washed over him again, settling in the region of his heart. Too much was going on, and he needed quiet time to analyze this new twist in his feelings. Maybe Jake had been right after all; maybe he did need quiet and isolation to get in touch with his old, stuck memories.

"You look... different," Laura said, taking the photos and arranging them on top of the dresser. "Are you okay?"

Shrugging, Morgan looked around. "Yeah, I'm fine." He could feel her gaze on him, the question strung between them. "Maybe a little tired," he said. Actually, that wasn't a lie. The trip by Learjet—his company jet, or so they told him—had been long and wearing on him. He twisted to look in her direction.

"I just heard the Jeep leave."

"Yes, Rachel's gone." Laura shrugged a little nervously. "It's just you and me now."

Morgan saw the exhaustion in her eyes. "Listen, why don't you rest? I can see you're tired."

"I'll be okay. Just being here is invigorating, isn't it?" She turned, covering her exhaustion with a strained smile.

Morgan had the crazy urge to step up to her, grab her by her small shoulders and give her a shake. She was putting on that cheery-faced routine for him again, and he could sense her retreating deep within herself—as usual. Keeping in mind Jake's warning that it was time to think of someone besides himself, he said gruffly, "When I saw those photos, I felt something...."

Laura's heart thudded once to underscore her reaction. "You did?"

With a shrug, Morgan growled, "I don't know what I felt. Just... something."

Looking around the room, Laura said, "Ann was hoping that if we got off alone, your memory might slowly begin to return."

Sunlight lanced through the western window of the bedroom, and Morgan saw it touch Laura's hair, the strands turning radiant, like a halo across her crown, until a breeze outside the cabin moved the branches of a pine tree and blocked the ray of light. How beautiful Laura was, he realized, beginning to appreciate her on a new, unspoken level. Her skin was translucent, and he could see the small blue veins beneath her eyes. Her mouth was decidedly one of her finest features—full and soft and excruciatingly vulnerable looking. He found himself wondering what it would be like to explore it with his own—and groaned internally at the thought.

The thought was so unbidden, so foreign to him, that Morgan stood very still, assimilating the urge. Scowling, he said, "Rachel mentioned that this used to be an area sacred to the Indians."

"Magic?" Laura said wistfully, beginning to put her clothes in the drawers. "We could use some magic in our lives right now," she added with a gentle laugh.

Morgan moved around the small room, noting that Laura's bed was no more than six feet from his. Beyond this room, a long, rectangular living room held a worn leather couch with a black-white-and-gray Navajo rug thrown over the back, and two overstuffed chairs. Although the cabin had electricity and running water, Oak Creek Canyon was several thousand feet deep, so television reception wasn't possible.

Morgan halted in the bedroom doorway, his hand resting tentatively on the jamb. Funny, he'd never studied Laura as he did now. She had an undeniable grace about her, in the way her small hands moved as she unpacked her clothes. Morgan liked the fact that she didn't wear much makeup or paint her fingernails. No, Laura had a distinctly natural quality. "You belong out here," he said huskily.

"What?" Laura straightened and looked up at him. The expression on Morgan's face was thoughtful, and Laura couldn't quite decipher the emotion banked in his darkened eyes. Her skin prickled pleasantly; a familiar sensation from the old days when he'd often fixed her with that hooded, burning look. Her mouth went dry momentarily, and she froze beneath his gaze.

Morgan watched Laura's eyes widen—beautifully. Could a change of location suddenly make him aware of her on such a new, primal level? He felt his body tighten with need—of her. The sensation was startling, and he wondered obliquely if she realized he wanted her sexually. That would be embarrassing—to her and him. He still didn't remember anything specific, but suddenly, his body was recalling something—something he had to fight. Morgan would no more entertain the thought of taking Laura for sexual reasons than he would any other woman. He had to feel more than raw, sexual chemistry.

"Uh..." He lifted his hand, a little embarrassed. "This place, I guess. I feel different here. How about you?"

Laura felt the invisible cord that had suddenly bound them snap and dissolve just as quickly as it had appeared. That intangible connection was an old,

wonderful feeling that had inexplicably established itself between them for the first time since Morgan's
return, however briefly. Once they'd shared that sensation twenty-four hours a day. Startled by its unexpected reemergence, Laura's voice was husky with
emotion as she said, "Yes, there's a feeling about this
place I can't put my finger on—yet."

Morgan saw her hands tremble slightly as she tucked
her silky lingerie away in the drawer. What would
Laura look like dressed in that pink silk camisole and
bikini panties? The image wavered tauntingly before
his eyes. With a shake of his head, he forced himself
away from the doorway and into the living room.
Looking down, he realized his body was responding to
her with a will of its own. Damn!

Feeling the need of fresh air, he went outside. A
battered four-wheel drive Toyota Land Cruiser sat
beside the cabin—their transportation if they needed
to go somewhere, though Major Houston had warned
them not to go anywhere without checking in with him
at ranch headquarters first. The old gray Toyota had
seen better days. As Morgan stepped onto the pine
needles, still damp from a rain two days earlier, he felt
a certain affinity with the vehicle. He was a little beat
up and rusty himself.

"Do you mind if I join you?"

Laura's voice intruded gently on his thoughts. It reminded him of the breeze wafting through the pine
trees that surrounded the log cabin. He'd jammed his
hands into his jeans pockets as he'd stood looking at
the Toyota. Now he looked across his shoulder to see
her standing tentatively, as if he might banish her with

a dark look or irritable wave of his hand. Her face was so easily read, her eyes broadcasting anxiety.

Morgan turned and gestured for her to come closer. "Let's go explore the creek."

"Are—are you sure?"

He studied her flushed face and gazed deeply into her eyes. Maybe this place really was magic, Morgan thought, as he felt Laura's anxiety, and sensed that she didn't want to be left alone—that she needed his company. His or anyone's? Rubbing his mouth with the back of his hand, he turned toward her fully. "Ann said I should try talking more openly to you," he confided in a low tone, "and I know I'm not the world's most talkative person. I feel you're anxious. Over what?"

Laura stood transfixed by his gray gaze. Morgan's face had changed from that frighteningly implacable mask to the familiar expression of the man she had known for so many years. Hungrily, she took in his concern—for her. It was the first time she'd experienced his care since his return, and it left her off balance and feeling suddenly vulnerable in a new way. Just as quickly, Morgan could close up, she knew, striking another wounding blow to her vulnerability. She wasn't sure she could stand too many more of those blows.

Opening her hands, she whispered, "I'm feeling pretty shaky right now, Morgan. I—" she looked up at the towering pine trees behind him "—my heart's beating like a runaway freight train in my chest and my hands are sweaty...."

Scowling, he moved slowly toward her. He not only heard but felt an edge of panic to her voice. Though he wanted to reach out and grip her hands, he stopped about six feet away. Yes, fear was mixed with the anxiety in her eyes. "I'm not too good at this yet," he mumbled, "about talking or trying to talk. What are you afraid of?"

Shrugging, Laura whispered, "I don't know. I really don't know." She rubbed her damp palms self-consciously on the thighs of her Levi's. Her heart continued to pound, and she wondered obliquely if she was having a heart attack. "I have to sit down," she said, and she moved spasmodically toward an old, carved bench along the cabin wall. If she didn't sit down, she feared her knees would buckle.

Without thinking, Morgan gripped her arm and guided her to the bench. Her skin was soft and firm beneath his hand. For a moment, the fragrance of her camellia perfume beckoned to him. He saw the flash of surprise in her eyes as he made contact and realized this was the first time he'd touched her. Once she was settled on the bench, he released her and crouched in front of her, a few inches separating them. Laura nervously touched her brow and tried to give him a smile that said she was going to be all right.

"Were you always like this?" he wondered in a low voice.

"Like what?" Laura asked, clasping her hands in her lap. Morgan's very presence was beckoning powerfully to her. Oh, to throw herself into his strong, capable arms and be held! How many times had she dreamed he was holding her safe? Holding her tight against his comforting bulk? Laura fought against those needs. Morgan had touched her because she was unsteady on her feet. It meant nothing personally to him, she realized with renewed agony.

Morgan gestured to her. "You always try to hide how you're really feeling. I can see you're scared about something."

Hanging her head, Laura closed her eyes. "It's— just a reaction. Ann told me they were called anxiety attacks."

"Why do you have them?"

Her throat closed with tears. She'd gotten so used to Morgan not caring about her personally that his unexpected focus was too much for her to cope with on top of her weakened state. "I—I've had them since my rescue," she stammered.

Morgan saw her wrestling with very real anxiety. Her hands twisted in her lap and the corners of her mouth pulled inward as if to battle inner demons. "Laura?" He called her name huskily, stunned by the avalanche of feeling behind it. But Morgan didn't have time to analyze his own responses. Right now, what was important was the fact that Laura was hurting.

Compressing her lips, Laura looked up—and nearly melted beneath Morgan's tender gaze. She wanted to fly off that bench and into his arms. Just to feel safe, even for a moment! "Ann calls it PTSD—Post Traumatic Stress Disorder." Her voice broke, and she forced out the rest of the words. "Anxiety attacks are part of it." She shrugged helplessly. "I don't get them very often. I don't know why I had one now. I—I feel safe here." She looked away. "I feel safe because you're here...."

As Morgan continued to crouch before her, he felt a gutting, knifelike sensation pierce his chest and move outward, as if someone were invisibly carving his heart into pieces. He saw Laura's courage in that moment, as she struggled to tame those demons that were strangling the life out of her eyes. "You might look fragile," he rasped, "but you sure as hell have courage." When she turned her head aside to avoid his gaze, Morgan slowly unwound from his position.

"Come on," he ordered huskily, holding out his hand to her. "What do you say we go for a walk and look around our new home?"

Chapter Five

Laura stared in disbelief as Morgan offered her his hand. It was a large, square hand, familiar old scars mingling with frightening new ones. Choking back a sob, she hesitantly lifted her hand and slid it into his. As his callused fingers curled around hers, she felt his momentary hesitation. He was doing this not because he'd suddenly rediscovered his love for her. No, it was a humane gesture, and she knew she had to be careful not to make anything more of it than that.

Still, as she stood, a thrill arced through her. Morgan's hand was as warm and dry as hers was damp and cool. Just the fact that he had made physical contact with her gave her the strength to stand. Her shaky knees grew stronger. Her heart rate slowed. All the while, her gaze was held by his tender one. It was as if so much of the old Morgan from before the kidnappings had returned to her side! Laura wanted to tell him, but the words wouldn't come.

Starved for the feel of him, she closed her eyes and merely stood there for a moment, savoring Morgan on all levels. The singing of the birds, the rush and tumble of the nearby creek, the soft breeze lifting her hair, all ceased to exist as she centered her heart and soul on his warm fingers curved around her own. She swore she could feel his pulse beat though his fingers, as if he were a lifeline restoring her will to live, feeding her with the desire to fight back for what had been so cruelly torn from her months before. She felt his strength infusing her, halting the terrible downward spiral she'd been inhabiting far too long.

In moments, the anxiety was washed away, replaced by a feeling of serenity that Laura had thought she'd never feel again. Morgan stood near her, mere inches between them as he lightly grasped her hand. He'd reached out to touch her of his own accord, not because she'd begged him to.

Morgan's hand disengaged from hers, and Laura's lashes flew open. To her regret, he moved away from her to follow a small path that led down to the creek bank. Tears welled into her eyes, and a cry lodged in her throat. She swayed, caught herself, then wrestled with the feeling of abandonment he'd created by releasing her. She stared at him, the cotton shirt stretched tautly across his massive shoulders as he picked his way carefully among the rocks and over downed tree limbs toward the creek's pebble-strewn bed. A breeze momentarily wafted several strands of his short, black hair.

Swallowing hard, Laura released a tremulous sigh. Well, what did she expect? Too much, she warned herself as she forced herself to follow him. Her steps seemed wooden and uncoordinated as she tried to recover from his fleeting touch, and her fingers tingled wildly where he'd held them. Heat throbbed moltenly upward through her arm to wrap softly around her aching heart. It was enough. Her heart was no longer bounding, and her anxiety had miraculously dissolved. For that she was more than grateful.

Laura tried to shift her focus and allow the healing beauty of Oak Creek Canyon to soothe her senses. Sunlight danced through pine boughs, dappling the bare, white branches of the gigantic sycamores that followed the curve of the bank. Morgan had found a large, oval sandstone boulder at the water's edge and taken a seat on it. She absorbed his rugged profile as he sat, legs drawn up, his massive arms encircling his knees.

Noting the unhappy line of his mouth, she realized that he, too, was suffering in his own private hell. What had it cost him to reach out to her? No longer did she ask herself each time something happened if an old memory from their past had jogged loose. Her hope on that score had been savagely reduced with every passing minute since his return. The psychiatrists said his memory was gone—forever. Only Dr. Parsons held out a ten-percent chance that some of it might be intact. But which parts? The Marine Corps experiences? The loss of his entire company on that hill in Vietnam? His years in the French Foreign Legion? Or—her fingers curled at her sides as she carefully made her way toward him—his memories of her, their family and their seven wonderful years together?

Life was so tenuous, Laura decided as she halted by the smooth sandstone boulder where Morgan sat. He turned his head, his gaze penetrating her like a laser. Laura felt the scorching quality of his eyes. When he looked at her like that, her entire body responded to him. How she ached to kiss him now that he was conscious. She was sure he didn't remember her kisses when he'd first roused from the coma.

"Sit down," he invited quietly.

Laura didn't sit too close to Morgan, although a healthy part of her cried out to do that very thing. He'd gestured where she should sit, so she did. It would do no good to crowd him. In fact, it might do more harm than good. Laura knew she couldn't make Morgan love her. She had to let him make the moves, no matter how hard it was not to reach out and tousle his hair or throw her arms around him as she would have before the kidnapping.

The boulder was sun-warmed, and Laura enjoyed the feel of it as she sat a foot away from Morgan, her legs crossed, her hands resting on her thighs. In front of them, Oak Creek, about a hundred feet wide and perhaps eight to ten feet deep, flowed strongly. The water was clear and she could see white, red, gray, yellow and black stones shimmering in the depths of the rushing cascade as it funneled, bubbled and frothed around the few larger boulders scattered along the creek bed.

Closing her eyes, she lifted her face to the late-afternoon sun. Soon it would dip behind the canyon walls on its winter orbit, and the boulder would become shaded. For now the sunlight warmed her cold, cold soul, and she reveled in the creek's laughing burble and the chirping of many birds she couldn't identify. For now, she decided, just feeling Morgan's nearness was enough.

Laura was aware of his magnificent bulk; much of the weight he'd lost was quickly returning. Morgan possessed a vibrancy she had always been aware of— and learned to depend on. She wondered if he was aware of his masculine vitality and decided he probably wasn't. So much of Morgan's life revolved around his company—worrying about his mercenary teams and their missions rather than himself or his personal needs.

"What are you thinking about?" he asked.

Laura smiled softly, her eyes remaining closed. Morgan's voice was husky and intimate. "I was thinking of you, of how deeply you care for other people before yourself."

Morgan scowled and played absently with a small pine branch he'd picked up on his way to the boulder. "How do you mean?"

A breeze caressed her, and her lips parted as she pretended it was Morgan reaching out for her. "You always cared deeply for others, Morgan. I think after you lost your men in Vietnam, you made a promise to yourself to never again allow anyone you had responsibility for to die." She opened her eyes and turned her head in his direction. His eyes were a smoky gray, and she knew he was thinking about what she'd said. "The guilt you felt over the loss of those men's lives has always been with you," she continued gently. "There were nights, after we were married, when you'd be up all night, pacing in our living room, worried about some team you'd sent out on a dangerous mission."

"I'd wake you up?"

Laura turned and faced him, careful to maintain the distance between them. "I pretended to be asleep, but I always woke up when you left my side." She smiled sadly and ran her fingertip across a tiny crevice in the boulder between them. "I knew you didn't want me up with you. You worried about waking me. When we first married, your PTSD symptoms were obvious. You had insomnia and bad nightmares and would toss and turn all night. At first you wouldn't let me sleep with you, but I persisted."

"What happened when I did?"

Laura met his somber gaze. "You started sleeping better."

"I see...."

"Holding someone you love can be healing," Laura said.

"I guess so." Morgan stared bleakly down at the small branch in his hands. He'd been stripping the bark from it systematically. "So, I'd get up and pace all night because I was worried about my employees?"

"Yes. And—" Laura drew up her legs, putting her arms around her knees "—when it was a really bad mission and you were particularly worried, you'd stay at the office. Sometimes I wouldn't see you at home with us for two or three days."

He stared at her. "I can't imagine being away from you for that long." The words came out of nowhere and Morgan stared at Laura, surprised by his own admission. He saw her eyes flare with equal surprise, then grow a misty blue as tears formed. Looking away, he suffered for her. He hadn't slept with her since coming out of the coma. Nor could he.

"I don't know where that came from," he said gruffly, tossing the stick into the stream.

Laura self-consciously dashed away the tears, her heart swelling with incredible joy at what he'd said. "You used to come home after a two- or three-nighter like that, and I'd be in bed. First you'd check on the kids. Then you'd come in, sit on my side of the bed, and..." Her voice faltered. She felt Morgan's gaze burning through her. "And you'd run your fingers through my hair." She fingered strands of hair at her temple. "I used to love your touching my hair like that. It was a wonderful way to wake up. You always loved to touch my hair. Often you'd brush it for me at night before we turned in.

"Sometimes when you came back after being gone for a while, I'd awaken and turn over. You'd put your arm around me and lean over and tell me you were crazy to stay away so long from me...from us...."

"Were you upset when I was gone like that?" Morgan held her dreamy gaze. He ached to reach out and untangle her thick blond hair from its ponytail. Some internal knowing was driving him, and for the first time, he began to understand what Dr. Parsons meant about feeling his way back into his lost memories. Something inside him knew his pleasure in brushing Laura's hair—and hers in having him do it.

"No. I understood your need to be with your people, to keep them safe. I know you would never have forgiven yourself if something happened and you weren't there. Even if a team was half a world away, you wanted to be as close to them as possible when danger threatened." She smiled softly. "That's one of the many things I've loved about you—your loyalty and care for others. I used to worry when you first created Perseus, because you'd go through such angst whenever you sent a team on a mission." She looked down at the boulder. "We had many, many discussions about your fears, your feelings, and how they were affecting us and the children."

Morgan digested Laura's admissions. It was the first time she'd talked intimately to him about the details of their former life together. Before, she'd limited herself to small talk with no real substance behind it. He dragged in a deep, ragged breath and continued to study Laura's profile as she watched the water rushing over the rocks in front of them. Jake was right: it was time to focus his attention on someone other than himself. Obviously, the old Morgan had attempted that care in a way he wasn't. Morgan wasn't sure what might have caused the change.

"Sitting here with you," he began in a low tone, "and talking like this, feeds me. I feel like I've been missing something. Starving for something I couldn't define—didn't know existed." He shook his head, unable to continue. This was what he'd been missing, he realized. He lifted his head and stared at Laura long and hard. *It was her.*

Laura felt heat tunnel through her like a beam of pure sunlight shafting through her heart at Morgan's words. His eyes were very clear now, a pale gray that told her how deeply he was forging a link with her. She not only saw it, she felt it. Something *was* happening. The old Morgan she knew and loved so fiercely was here now with her, even if he didn't realize that what he missed was her. Did she dare hope some small bit of their connection had survived the trauma he'd endured? That alert, hawklike gaze, that invisible energy that now swirled and danced around her, making her feel as if she was the very center of his universe, like a healing unguent to the psychic wounds she'd sustained throughout the past three months.

And Laura began to understand what had helped forge the link once again between them: her honest sharing of the tiny, daily details that had made up the fabric of their life together. Trying to quell her excitement at the discovery, she said in a husky tone, "There were nights that you'd come home, Morgan, and you'd be completely exhausted. You'd tousle my hair and wake me up, and I could see the dark circles under your eyes. Sometimes you hadn't shaved in days, and sometimes I knew you'd been crying."

Laura hesitated and slowly stroked the boulder's smooth surface with her fingers, fighting the insane urge to reach out and stroke Morgan's skin. "I knew if I awoke and saw your red-rimmed eyes, something had gone very wrong. I'd get up, and we'd go to the kitchen, and I'd make tea. I would watch you wrestle with your pent-up emotions. One part of you wanted to cry out your pain and loss, while the other part, the military part, would try to jam the sorrow and tears deep down inside. I'd ask you about the mission, about what had happened. Little by little, I'd see you stop gripping the mug in front of you, and I'd see the tears start slowly forming in your eyes.

"I would get up, put my cup down on the table and come to your side. Usually, I'd press your head against me, put my arms around you and just hold you. I'd gently touch your hair. Then I'd feel this awful struggle begin within you. I'd feel a sob wanting to tear free, but you'd fight it with everything you had. Finally, you'd trust me enough, and you'd bury your head against me, wrap your arms around me and cry." She pressed her lips together and held his gaze. "You'd cry long and hard because someone you had known, someone you'd wanted to keep safe, had died."

Laura continued to stroke the stone absently, lost in the memories, closing her eyes as she shared them with him. "I'd rock you and hold you. You were so strong that sometimes I was afraid you would squeeze me in two, you held me so tightly...."

Taking in a ragged breath, she whispered, "Afterward, we'd go to the master bathroom. We have a Jacuzzi in there, and I'd take off your clothes and get you in that hot, bubbling water. Water has always had a healing effect on you, Morgan. I would get you in there, sponge you down and we'd...well, we'd relax...."

In that instant, Morgan knew that he'd made love with Laura at those times. He saw the shyness in her face, heard it in her whispered tone as a pink flush stained her cheeks. She was staring down at her hand on the rock, unable to meet his gaze.

An intense, burning sensation began to coil and tighten in his lower body. How he ached to love Laura! But from his perspective, it was a physical attraction he didn't dare indulge. She deserved so much more. Frustrated, he watched the slight, inconstant breeze move tendrils of her blond hair against her flushed cheeks. He wanted to reach out and touch those golden strands, run his scarred fingertips across the slope of her cheek. What did Laura's skin feel like? Was it as soft as her voice, which reminded him of a summer's breeze? Was it as velvet as it looked? Aching to find out, and knowing it would only raise unfair hope in her, he jammed his hands between his crossed legs.

"It sounds," he said, groping to find the right words, "as if we had a pretty close relationship."

Laura smiled brokenly and moved her hand gently across the rock. "Yes—we did."

"And it sounds like I got a hell of a lot from it. But what did I ever do for you?"

Laura smiled to herself. She lifted her head and met his burning, nearly colorless gaze. "When I got hit by that car at National Airport, you were an absolute stranger, and you rode in the ambulance to the hospital and hung around until I became conscious." She opened her hands and gave him a strained smile. "Maybe that's what I love about the military so much, Morgan, I don't know. Maybe that's why I worked within that industry, because my father was a marine. Even though I was adopted, he had a kind of loyalty to my mother and me that I saw didn't often exist out in the civilian world. I grew up feeling very loved and cared for.

"When I awoke in the hospital—blind—and you came in, I knew in my heart everything was going to be all right." She touched her eyes with her fingers. "I was scared to death not being able to see. Nothing like that had ever happened to me before. My parents were dead by then. I had no one, but suddenly there you were, bigger than life, coming into that room, grabbing my hand and telling me you weren't going to leave me."

Morgan saw the warmth and tenderness in Laura's eyes. He felt it like a glowing fire kindled within him, making his heart swell in some unknown but powerful emotional knowing. Though he had no conscious memory of what she was telling him, he felt a strange sort of inner connection to the incident. "What happened next?"

Laura smiled fondly. "I hate hospitals—like you— and I wanted to leave. The doctor got angry and said I had to remain under observation for at least two days. You saw my need to go home and understood that at home, I'd feel safe and be able to recover more quickly."

"So I took you home." He shook his head. "I'm amazed you'd trust a complete stranger like that."

With a small laugh, Laura dangled her legs over the edge of the boulder. She gave him an impish look. "You still don't get it to this day, Morgan. You didn't at the time, and after we were married, I tried to make you understand, but you just didn't."

"What didn't I understand?" He liked the way her eyes were dancing with a childlike delight. It was good to see her lips curve upward. Something about her laughter, her smile, made him feel damn good about being a man and being with her.

"Your effect on me. On everyone. You're completely oblivious to it, Morgan. You forge an immediate bond of trust with anyone who comes in contact with you, and you don't even realize it. It's the mark of a natural leader. That's why you were so good in the

Marine Corps and the French Foreign Legion. People trust you. We instinctively know you'll go through hell and back for us. We sense it, and if we're privileged enough to be around you, we see it in action every day, in large and small ways.

"You didn't abandon me—or take advantage of me—in my darkest hour of need, Morgan. You took me home, nursed me and cared for me. You took care of my baby robin that had fallen from its nest, and you took care of Sasha, my Saint Bernard. To me—" she smiled gently over at him "—you're like a big old teddy bear, the kind you can cuddle up to and hold and feel safe with."

His mouth quirked. "A teddy bear, huh?"

Laughing lightly, Laura nodded. "You gave Jason one shortly after he was born, and when Katherine Alyssa came, she got one, too. Didn't you know? That bears are healers who protect their own?"

"No..." He stared down at his hands. The sun slid slowly past the canyon rim and he felt an immediate drop in temperature. Laura wasn't wearing a jacket, and although he was still comfortable, he wondered if she was. Rousing himself, he said, "Let's get back to the cabin. It's going to get dark pretty soon."

Laura swallowed her disappointment. She shivered and wrapped her arms around herself after she slid off the rock. Waiting, she watched Morgan move a lot more slowly from his perch. She knew from Dr. Parson's examination that he had been so badly tortured that even his joints, especially his knees, were still healing. He reminded her of a huge football player who had been in too many games, and never been given the time or care to recover sufficiently from all those powerful, bruising hits.

Swallowing hard, Laura decided not to wait for him. Maybe he would read her waiting the wrong way. Right now, they'd just forged a link between them for the first time, and she didn't want it destroyed by some mistake on her part. As she carefully picked her way through the pebbled area, she hoped she wouldn't accidentally slam the door shut on what they'd just achieved. She had no manual to follow on how to handle this situation, and right now she was extremely fearful of making a mistake.

The cabin was cool. An earth stove stood in one corner, and she saw that someone had thoughtfully placed a box of chopped wood nearby so they could start a fire. The living room was long and rectangular, and the dull shine of the pine floor complemented the brown leather couch and forest green chairs.

"Will you start a fire?" she asked Morgan as he entered. "I'll go look in the fridge and see what Rachel left for dinner."

He nodded. "Sure, go ahead." Closing the door, he watched Laura move to the kitchen. She seemed happier. Or was it his imagination? He felt happier. Why? Because of their intimate conversation on the rock? Possibly. It was the first time they'd been able to sit down and really talk. Moving to the stove, he opened the door and wadded up a bunch of newspapers, deep in thought.

What were they going to do tonight—with one bedroom and two beds less than six feet apart? His sleep had been light and sporadic in the hospital. As he placed wood in the stove, his frown deepened. Part of him, a very primal part, considered Laura's proximity strictly on a physical level. How he wanted to love her! Did she realize how peaceful he felt in her sunny presence? She fed him in some invisible way he couldn't explain. His body knew and was in a constant, aching knot, obviously recalling a great deal more than his damned brain did about Laura and how he felt toward her.

Lighting the fire, Morgan slowly eased upright and watched the tongues of flame lick eagerly at the wood. That was how he felt toward Laura: like a blazing flame wanting to lick and touch every inch of her skin. He wanted to taste her, feel the pressure of her lips against his, tunnel his fingers through her thick blond hair and then...

Making a sound of disgust, Morgan slammed shut the stove door and jammed his hands into the pockets of his jeans. What the hell was the matter with him? Where was this high-minded concern for others that Laura had spoken so well of? His reasons for wanting Laura were far from high-minded. No, they were strictly selfish.

Chapter Six

Laura emerged from the tiny bathroom in a pink flannel nightgown falling to her ankles, covered by a white chenille robe. She carried her brush. The hot bath had been reviving, and she touched her cheek, which felt warm and flushed, as she padded out into the living room where Morgan was reading.

The cabin was pleasantly warm from the heat thrown out by the stove. A sense of peace filled Laura as she halted in the doorway. Morgan sat on the couch, newspaper in hand, deep in concentration. Little by little, as the evening had passed, he had truly begun to relax, and for that Laura was supremely grateful. Dinner had been somewhat stilted, but afterward, when she took out her needlepoint and sat in the living room, leaving him alone, he'd eventually come in and sat down, too.

A tender smile pulled at her mouth now as she absorbed the sight of him sitting so peacefully. Moving into the room, she lowered herself to sit on a thick sheep's fleece in front of the hearth. Leaning her back against the chair closest to the rug, she slowly began to brush her hair. She felt more than saw Morgan shift his attention to her.

Morgan scowled as he felt Laura's presence. When she walked past him, he automatically inhaled deeply, and the scent of orange blossoms filled his flaring nostrils. Laura looked thin in the nightgown and robe, and the observation struck him hard. Always before, he'd seen her in a dress or suit, bulky winter clothes that disguised her thinness. He frowned.

"You're skinny as a rail," he growled, laying the newspaper aside.

Laura stopped brushing her hair for a moment. Morgan was studying her darkly, his hands clasped between his thighs. "Skinny?"

"Yes."

Smiling slightly, she began to brush her hair again. "I lost twenty pounds or so, as you did," she said softly.

With each stroke of the brush, Morgan felt an aching need grow within him. Laura was so incredibly graceful, her face serene—in sharp contrast with his burgeoning emotions. The little makeup she'd worn was gone, replaced with the fresh-scrubbed look of a college girl. Morgan found it tough to believe that Laura had borne two children. His children, he reminded himself awkwardly. Her hair glinted molten gold in the lamplight, the shadows gently shaping her clean features. Yes, Laura was beautiful to him.

Forcing his gaze down to his hands, he said grimly, "You didn't eat enough for a bird tonight at dinner."

"No..."

"Why not?" He'd eaten like a lumberjack. Laura had prepared steaks, a mountain of fried potatoes, steamed broccoli, and homemade garlic toast. The food, his first real meal since being released from the damn hospital, had tasted delicious. But halfway through the meal he'd realized she was merely picking at her steak, cutting it into smaller and smaller pieces but not eating much of consequence. He hadn't said anything at the time, but seeing now how gaunt she actually was, he couldn't remain silent.

Placing the brush in her lap, Laura stared down at it. The tortoise shell object, which had once belonged to her mother, was smooth and comforting in her hands. "I—don't know, Morgan."

"People don't eat because they're upset, or something's bothering them."

"I suppose that's true."

"So what's bothering you?"

His abruptness was like a physical blow to her, and Laura felt herself wince at his question. Nervously, she turned the brush in her hands. "I really haven't felt like eating since the kidnappings, Morgan."

"But we're all back now. We're safe. You should be eating more."

Struggling against anger and hurt, Laura lifted her chin and met his flat, searching stare. How like Morgan to address the issue so bluntly, with no preamble. He wasn't known for his diplomacy, and he certainly wasn't showing any here, with her. "*You* might feel safe enough—emotionally stable enough—to resume your normal eating patterns.''

"You're saying you don't feel safe?"

Hot tears flooded Laura's eyes, and she looked away from him. Her voice grew strained. ''Morgan, you forget that I'm still trapped.'' She forced herself to look at him. ''I don't have a husband. The man who used to love me is still lost to me. I-I'm alone, Morgan, and when I try to eat, I feel nauseous.''

Her words carved pain into his chest. He bowed his head, unable to hold her anguished look. The line of Laura's lips told him how much she was fighting not to cry in front of him, and he felt like hell—as if all this was his fault. Angry at hurting her, because she didn't deserve that kind of pain, he abruptly got to his feet.

"Go to bed," he said gruffly, then turned and walked stiffly out of the room toward the bathroom.

"Damn . . ." Laura whispered tautly, her fingers clenched tightly on the brush. She heard the bathroom door shut a little more loudly than was necessary. What could she have said differently so as not to upset Morgan? She was at a loss. Maybe she should have lied. No, that wasn't right, either. With a sigh, she got to her feet and went into the bedroom.

Laura chose the bed nearest the window. How could she possibly sleep with Morgan so close to her? Placing the brush on the dresser, she eased out of her robe and laid it across the foot of her bed. Fatigue lapped at her, and as she snuggled down beneath the covers, she realized she might fall asleep anyway. The flight had been long, and travel in general always sapped her energy for a day or two.

As her head sunk into the pillow, she closed her eyes. The wool blanket was scratchy against her neck, but she didn't care. Exhaustion stalked her. As she felt herself spiraling downward toward badly needed sleep, she made a mental note to call Susannah Killian tomorrow morning and talk to her, and then to Jason. She worried how he was getting along. Katherine was too young to realize what had happened, so Laura felt easier about her. Vaguely, she heard the shower running. Morgan must be washing up. It was the last coherent thought she had as sleep dragged her deep within its embrace.

Morgan ruefully rubbed his damp hair with a towel as he quietly entered the bedroom. The lukewarm shower had felt good on the healing wounds on his back from whippings he couldn't remember. He'd stood under the shower nearly half an hour, letting the water slough away his anger and frustration. Just being able to bathe so luxuriously was like a gift to him.

The light from the living room cascaded silently into the bedroom. He halted just inside the door, taking in the way the light slid across the pine floor and up and across Laura's bed, making burnished gold of her lightly tousled hair. Dropping the towel on the dresser, Morgan ran his fingers distractedly through his own damp strands. His gaze was focused on Laura—and so was his body.

How beautiful she was, he thought as he quietly padded to the side of her bed. He placed his hands in the pockets of the dark blue terry-cloth robe he wore, afraid of reaching out and touching that thick, cascading hair. Her lips were gently parted, one hand beneath her cheek as she slept, and the covers had slipped down to reveal her small but proud shoulder covered by the pink flannel nightgown.

As he stood looking at her, Morgan began to realize how stress affected Laura. She had beautiful, well-placed cheekbones, but her skin was stretched tautly across them, and bluish purple shadows showed beneath her eyes even in sleep. Her breathing was soft and shallow. Though aching to reach out and touch her hair, to see if it really felt as silky as it looked, Morgan forced himself to step away and take off his robe.

Beneath it he wore only blue-and-white striped pajama bottoms. If he weren't sleeping in the same room with Laura, he'd wear nothing at all. He didn't like clothes binding and twisting around his body as he slept. Wondering if the old Morgan had felt that way, he dropped the robe at the end of his bed. He pulled back the covers, then walked quietly into the living room and shut off the lights.

The darkness was complete, and he stood where he was for a moment, the soft crackle and snap of wood in the stove soothing his tense body. The rush of water in the creek outside the cabin filled him with an odd sense of peace. A feeling of safety wrapped around him as he padded back to the bedroom, his eyes now adjusted to the dark.

Even in the darkness, a thin slice of moon outside glimmered down to reveal the canyon's craggy cliffs. As he sat on the edge of his bed, his hands resting on his thighs, he saw the gentle moonglow envelop like a whitish halo about her still, sleeping form, caressing her features, silhouetting her full, parted lips and the thick lashes resting against her cheekbones. She slept deeply, and for some reason, that made Morgan feel good. Laura had said his presence helped her feel safe.

Warmth threaded through his heart at that realization as he sat watching her take slow, regular breaths. Faintly, he could detect the fragrance of the orange-blossom crystals she'd used in her bath. His mind gyrated back to the fact that Laura was thin. Too damned thin. He hadn't realized the depth of destruction this ordeal had wreaked on her until now—because he'd been too busy feeling sorry for himself and his lost memory, he reminded himself sulkily.

His gaze rested for a moment on the photos Laura had placed on the dresser—of their children and the rest of his family. Everything she was doing was for him, he realized. But what was Laura doing to help herself recover from the kidnapping? Angry that he hadn't even bothered to ask her what had happened during her imprisonment with Guillermo Garcia, Morgan promised her silently that he would try to repair that bridge between them in the next few days.

Hope came on the heels of his realizations. Unconsciously, Morgan rubbed his thickly haired chest. Something was miraculously at work within him that he couldn't quite define—yet. Still, it was there. Intuitively, he knew he had to follow those feelings, retaining an almost blind faith in believing that possibly, just possibly, part of his memory would return with it.

A ragged sigh escaped as he eased himself onto his bed. Hope was such a fragile, tentative thing. He saw it in Laura's eyes, heard it in her voice, all the time. As he pulled up the covers and turned on his side, facing her, he closed his eyes. Morgan had no idea if he'd sleep or not. Having Laura this close to him was a new experience, and he didn't quite trust himself because he wanted her on such a selfish, primal level. It wasn't right, he told himself harshly. She was still recovering from her own terrible trauma. Determined to ask her about her experience with Garcia tomorrow, Morgan closed his eyes. In moments, he was asleep.

A whimper awakened Morgan, and he sat up instantly, his heart pounding, adrenaline heightening his senses. He'd heard a woman cry out. *Laura*. Jerking his attention to the left, he gazed over at her. She seemed fine.

He had no idea of the time. The sleep torn from him, he threw off his covers and sat up, the pine floor cold under his bare feet. The room was chilly—the fire in the stove had obviously gone out.

Rubbing his face to get reoriented, Morgan sat rigidly, wondering if he was having another nightmare. He'd heard Laura's cry—he'd swear he had. Yet she lay sleeping quietly. Or was she? It took more precious moments for him to come fully awake. His pulse was bounding. He felt and tasted fear. Why? As his gaze ruthlessly moved across Laura again, he realized something was wrong.

Her bed covers were twisted around her, and her nightgown had ridden up above her knees, bunching between the soft, white curve of her thighs. She was lying in a fetal position, her hands and arms pressed tightly against her. Her beautiful hair was tangled, and as he rose unsteadily to his feet to move to her side, Morgan realized she must have been thrashing her

head from side to side on her pillow to mess it up so
much.

Without thinking, he leaned over and pressed his
hand lightly to her shoulder. My God, her nightgown
was wringing wet! Scowling, he ran his hand down her
arm and felt a slight tremble, finally realizing she was
sleeping through a nightmare that held her tightly in
its grip. The once-soft line of her mouth was compressed, the corners pulled inward with pain.

When Morgan's fingers touched her lower arm, he
felt the cool dampness of her skin. She could catch her
death of pneumonia! Reaching down, he brought the
covers up and over her, tucking them in around her
shoulders. It was then he realized her breathing was
ragged and shallow, almost as if she were panting. A
moan tore from her lips, and she jerked her head to
one side.

Morgan eased himself down on the side of the bed,
his hip resting against her. He couldn't stand to hear
her whimper. Instinctively he stroked her hair and instantly her mouth lost some of its tension. Marveling
that something so small as a light touch could have so
much effect, he grew bolder. His heart felt as if it was
tearing from his chest as he watched Laura wrestle
with something he could neither see nor hear. What he
could see was its impact on her.

"It's all right, Laura," he rasped, gently tunneling
his fingers through her hair. "You're safe...safe...."
he crooned as he leaned over, his lips near her small,
delicate ear. Her hair felt like fine, strong silk to him.
The joy of getting to touch her thrilled him as nothing had since he'd awakened from the coma. Her hair

was thick and slightly curly, the strands yielding to his strokes, curving about his exploring fingers.

Morgan watched in amazement as her breathing began to slow and become more regular. He felt her whole body relax as he continued his gentle ministrations. Allowing his hand to move more boldly, he slipped it downward, across her blanketed shoulders. Her lips lost their tense line entirely and slowly parted. Good. How greatly he'd underestimated the importance of touch for a person in pain. Then he recalled Laura's admissions earlier this afternoon on the boulder about how she had held him and allowed him to cry against her.

His eyes glinted with tenderness as he absorbed the sight of her sleeping features. A powerful mixture of joy, gratitude and other, undefined emotions mushroomed through his chest. Just the act—the privilege—of touching Laura was more than enough for him right now, Morgan realized humbly. Before, he'd wanted her sexually. Now, at her bedside, tenderly touching her hair and back, he was filled with such a sense of peace that it shook him deeply.

Morgan loved the way her lips slowly parted to reveal their lush fullness. Trusting his feelings, he leaned over even farther, enough to touch her lips with his own. The moment his mouth met hers, something deep and powerful exploded within him, radiating outward through every inch of his body. Her lips were just as soft as he'd imagined. As he tasted their texture, he felt her move beneath him.

Panicked, he broke contact with her mouth, his hand automatically going back to her hair. He saw her thick eyelashes flutter and barely open, to reveal drowsy blue eyes.

"Go back to sleep, Laura," he rasped huskily. "You're safe...safe..."

Morgan watched her lids droop closed again. What was going on here? Just the guttural tone of his voice, certainly off-key, had soothed her. Laura snuggled her face into the pillow, a sigh slipping from her lips. Afraid to move, afraid she might wake up and discover him with her, Morgan remained sitting next to her for a good five minutes. But it was no longer torture but pure heaven to be here with her, his hand stilled on her thick hair, his hip pressed pleasantly against her now-relaxed body.

If there were such things as miracles—and Morgan didn't really believe in them—then this moment with Laura was as close as he'd probably ever get. It shook him that his touch and voice could have such a profound, healing effect on another human being. Laura was relaxed, her breathing slow and cadenced. Whatever nightmare she'd been inhabiting had fled. Somehow, in his blundering need to help her, he'd chased it away.

Slowly he eased his hand out of the tangle of her hair. He'd kissed her. He'd tasted her lips. Staring down at Laura, he wondered with panic if she would remember him stealing that kiss from her. And it was a stolen thing. Or was it? A part of him had responded to her out of selfish need. But another part had offered the kiss as—what? A healing gesture? With a shake of his head, Morgan cursed himself and slowly eased upward, hoping not to waken Laura. He stood over her a moment, watching her continue to sleep the sleep of angels. Because that was what she was—an angel in human form.

He smiled tenderly at the thought, wishing he had some of her patience, her gentleness and diplomacy. They were diametric opposites, he was beginning to discover, and as he made his way over to his bed, Morgan felt like a lump of hard black coal next to Laura, who shone like a diamond of light in his dark, complex world.

As he lay down and pulled up the covers, he saw the first gray streaks of dawn edging the top of the canyon. It must be around four or five o'clock. Closing his eyes, he centered hotly on the memory of Laura's lips beneath his. He'd kissed her carefully, lightly, their mouths barely touching, but it had been enough—for now. With that thought, he slid into a sleep heated by dreams of Laura, of loving her until she cried out with the unadulterated pleasure that he somehow knew only he could give her.

The smell of bacon frying, of coffee perking, slowly awakened Laura. At first she didn't realize where she was, because the sounds of the creek were so different from those around their Virginia home. She sat up, her hair tumbling in disarray around her face. Pushing several strands out of her eyes, she looked around. Sunlight cascaded through the bedroom window. It took her a long moment to realize she was at the Donovan Ranch, in a log cabin, and—Morgan!

Instantly, Laura looked to her right. The twin bed Morgan had slept in was a tangle of sheets and blankets. He was gone. Panic set in momentarily, and Laura threw off her covers, lowering her bare feet to the cool pine floor. Then, more gradually, she acknowledged the fragrance of breakfast cooking and realized Morgan must be up and making breakfast.

Her panic and anxiety dissolved as she sat running her fingers through her hair and laughing at her groggy state. Exhaustion still lapped at her, but for some reason, she felt better. Happier. Mornings weren't usually her strong point, so she stayed on the edge of the bed, allowing herself the luxury of waking up slowly. In the old days, she would have been out of bed by six, fixing Morgan's breakfast before he left for work. Then Jason would stumble out of his room around seven, his blue security blanket—"blankey"—in tow. He'd rub his little freckled face, his gray eyes sleepily trained on his father, who'd be at the kitchen table eating a healthy breakfast.

So many wonderful memories.... Laura sighed, closed her eyes and allowed them to surface within her. Jason loved to climb into his father's lap, blankey and all, and beg for a piece of bacon from Morgan. There they'd sit, Jason happily ensconced in Morgan's embrace, eating breakfast with Daddy. It was a precious time between father and son, and Laura had loved being privy to their bonding....

Somewhere in her groggy state, Laura vaguely recalled Morgan kissing her. He always kissed her after breakfast, and then Jason would lean forward and place his own wet kiss on her cheek. It was a breakfast ritual of sorts, Laura supposed. Morgan's kiss was always warm and tender—how she looked forward to it! She lightly touched her lower lip. The kiss...had she dreamed it? She frowned, trying to remember. Where did dreams end and reality begin? Had she dreamed of Morgan tunneling his fingers through her hair last night and then awakening her with a kiss? Or was it a wish-fulfillment figment of her overactive imagination?

Unsure, Laura again grazed her lower lip with her fingertips, thinking. Was she going crazy? In one part of her drowsy mind, she was sure Morgan had kissed her last night! But he wouldn't do that. With a frustrated sound, she decided the whole memory was nothing more than trying to make her agonizing need of him a reality—to return to the intimacy of before the kidnappings.

Easing off the bed, Laura felt depression settling once again around her shoulders. Maybe she was slowly going crazy, falling off some unknown precipice deep within herself, and just didn't realize it yet. Pulling open a dresser drawer, she listlessly chose some pink lingerie for the day, and added a peach-colored mohair sweater and dark blue slacks. No, it was her, she decided sadly as she picked up her sensible brown shoes and headed to the bathroom. Her and her overriding need for Morgan to remember his love for her and the two children that was pushing her toward that invisible precipice. Laura wondered bleakly if she could hold on long enough to help Morgan remember his past. She wasn't sure. Not at all.

Chapter Seven

Laura was so exhausted by her night's tossing and turning that it was impossible to erect any barriers against Morgan after her hot shower. She walked hesitantly to the kitchen to get some coffee and was surprised to see him looking well-rested, sitting at the round oak table, a mug of coffee in his hand. He wore a yellow-blue-and-purple plaid flannel shirt with his jeans—a definite departure from the old Morgan's preference for conservative colors.

"Good morning," she said, her voice still low with sleepiness.

Morgan watched Laura head for the the coffeemaker. "We survived the night. I think that's important," he said gruffly in greeting. Despite his good intentions, his body tightened with painful awareness of Laura. Her hip-length sweater gently outlined her breasts, slim torso and slightly rounded abdomen, and the slacks, though tapered, revealed her fine, long legs.

Laura poured a cup of coffee, struggling to hide her shaking hands from Morgan. The roughness of his voice grated on her exposed nerves. She noticed a plate of scrambled eggs and bacon sitting in the microwave.

"Is that for me?" she asked, pointing to it.

"Yeah. I can't guarantee they'll be any good, but you need someone around to put some meat on those bones. I'm willing to give it a try if you are."

A slight smile tugged at the corners of her mouth as she heated the breakfast. "This is something new," she murmured, leaning against the counter, the cup of coffee in her hands as she looked across the kitchen at him. "You never made me breakfast before. Maybe there's a positive side to the amnesia I overlooked." It was a poor joke, but she saw him rally—for her sake, she was sure—his lips curving slightly in response.

Her gaze settled on his mouth. Instantly, a flash of a memory sizzled through her. *Had* Morgan kissed her last night? How badly she wanted to ask, yet she didn't dare. Still, the tingling warmth settling in her belly suggested he had. Either that, or her nighttime dream world was becoming disturbingly real during the day. Fortunately, this was a good dream rather than a nightmare, and for that she was grateful.

"Come and sit down," Morgan invited as he slowly stood and pulled out a chair next to his. "You're the one who lost a lot of sleep last night...."

Laura frowned and moved toward him. "I was hoping we'd have separate bedrooms," she murmured, her voice strained.

"Why?" he demanded as she sat. "So I wouldn't know about your nightmares?"

Laura held herself stiffly, conscious of Morgan's bulk and warmth directly behind her chair. His large hands still rested on the chair back, his fingers barely grazing her shoulders. A part of her cried out for his direct touch. If only he could feel her suffering—her need for contact! Shakily, she set the mug of coffee down on the table before she spilled it.

"Dr. Parsons said it was part of the process," she whispered, her mouth going dry.

"Hmph," Morgan said, going to the microwave. He pulled out her breakfast plate and set it down in front of her. "Here, eat it. All of it. I'm making you two pieces of toast to go with it, and I want to see them go down the hatch, too."

Laura smiled tentatively as she looked at the plate, burdened with what must be at least four scrambled eggs. "Morgan," she protested, "there's enough food here for three men!"

He popped two slices of bread into the toaster. "So?" Turning, he saw the bewilderment written across her pale features. In that moment, he realized just how fragile Laura was. Old feelings and awareness moved strongly through him, and though he still couldn't call them memories, he knew the alarm he was experiencing was genuine. Even Laura's hair, barely tamed into some semblance of order, needed a good brushing. She wasn't taking the kind of care of herself she could be, he knew from some far recess deep within him.

"Well—" Laura waved her hands helplessly, looking at the fare "—it's so much!"

"Eat what you can," he said less gruffly, "and then we'll talk."

Talk about what? Laura wondered dully as she forced herself to pick up the fork and swallow some of the eggs. She could barely taste them, though she realized Morgan had gone to some trouble to sprinkle in bits of fresh parsley and chopped red pepper to make them more appealing and palatable. It was a thoughtful gesture on his part.

Just then, Morgan leaned forward and two pieces of thickly buttered toast appeared on her plate. "Eat these, too," he ordered, as he poured himself another cup of coffee and sat down opposite her.

A thread of happiness wound its way into Laura's depression as she force-fed herself at the kitchen table with Morgan looking on, his features unrelenting. A ray of sunlight filtered through the red-and-white checked curtains at the window. Chickadees chirped outside, and the creek was gurgling merrily, the sounds soothing to her frayed composure.

"While you're eating," Morgan continued in a more conversational tone, watching her closely, "I had a couple of fragmented dreams last night I wanted to share with you."

Laura stopped eating. "Have you had dreams before?"

"Not like these." Morgan gestured at the plate. "Keep eating or I don't talk."

She smiled a little. "This is blackmail, Morgan."

"Call it what you want. My heart's in the right place."

Hope rose briefly in her as she saw his clear gray eyes sparkle teasingly. Just the lowering of his voice was like a balm to her taut emotional state, healing her. She continued to eat, not wanting him to clam up. "Tell me about your dreams?" she asked.

He turned the cup slowly in his hands. "Since waking from the coma, I've gotten fragments of things—snatches of a voice saying something, a pair of eyes or a swatch of color of someone's hair." His brows fell. "Last night, after I got you settled from your nightmare, I went back to sleep. It was then I had these dreams. I should say, dream fragments."

Laura stared at him. Her fork halted halfway to her mouth. "I had a nightmare?" She had absolutely no memory of it. A deep caring burned in Morgan's eyes—caring for her—and she felt its healing power sink deep into her wounded spirit.

"Yeah," he muttered, "you had a nightmare, all right. We'll talk about it after you're done eating."

Laura shrugged. "I don't want to talk about it at all."

"You don't have that choice."

Laura's stomach churned. Her mouth went dry. "Why don't you tell me about your dreams?" she whispered, eager to hear about something better than her own rotten nightmares, which had haunted her since the kidnapping.

Opening his hands, Morgan said, "I remember a lot of cardboard boxes in a living room. They were draped with sheets. I saw three kids playing in them."

Laura straightened, her eyes widening. "Yes!"

He gave her a wary look. "Yes?"

Excitedly, Laura said, "When you, Aly and Noah were kids, you used to build cardboard 'cities' out of boxes in the living room." Her voice broke with joy.

"Oh, Morgan, that's a wonderful memory to have return! What else did you see?"

He shrugged, feeling her delight, seeing her once-wan cheeks turn bright pink and her blue eyes light up with hope. He grinned a little, elated that the fleeting image was a genuine memory from his past.

"So you didn't recognize the kids as you and your brother and sister?"

"No...it was like a movie, and I was watching it."

"Did you hear them speak?"

"No, I'm afraid not."

Unthinkingly, Laura reached over and gripped his arm. "Oh, Morgan, it's still wonderful! It's proof that at least part of your memory is intact." She felt his muscles respond instantly to her touch and saw an undefinable emotion pass through Morgan's eyes, leaving her shaken and needy in its wake. Hesitantly, Laura forced herself to release him. Trying to still her burgeoning happiness, she whispered, "What else did you dream?"

"I saw you," he said.

"Me?" Laura sat very still, afraid to breathe. "When?"

"I know you told me you were at an airport—that we met there when a car struck you," Morgan said. "But last night I saw you there and you were wearing a pink raincoat." He studied her intently. "Were you?"

A shattering bolt of joy flowed through her. "Yes, I was wearing a pink raincoat that day." Laura set her fork down and pressed her hands to her mouth, afraid she was going to cry in front of him. She knew how

Morgan hated to see her weep. Tears burned in her eyes and she blinked them away.

Morgan saw moisture glimmer in Laura's eyes for just a moment. He saw the utter joy written on her face, now radiant with hope. He felt her hope, too. Deep in his heart, he knew why these fragmented memories had surfaced. It was because of kissing her last night. Somehow, that kiss had unlocked the vault of his past. "I saw one other thing," he said gruffly, his voice emotional. "I was in a battle . . . bodies were lying all around me." His hands tightened around the mug. "I was on a hill above a jungle."

Sobering, Laura dropped her hands in her lap. "I'm sure it was the hill where your company was overrun," she whispered, aware of the pain in his voice and face. "In some ways, I wished certain memories from your past would never resurface, Morgan. They were so terrible . . . and I'm not sure how you came to grips with the guilt you carried from them. I don't think I could have." Reaching out, she placed her hand over his. Tightening her fingers, she said, "Still, those memories are real, and they are a part of your past. I can hardly wait to tell Dr. Parsons."

Morgan curved his fingers around her cool, damp ones in return. Laura had eaten barely a quarter of the food on her plate. "Hold on," he ordered, "let's just wait and see what else happens before we go running to Dr. Parsons."

Somberly, Laura nodded. Morgan's hand was warm and felt so good to her. She was thrilled he was returning her heartfelt touch. "Okay, we'll wait."

"Right now," he said, removing the plate from in front of her, "we need to talk about you...about your nightmare."

Stiffening, Laura pulled her hand out of his. "I don't remember it, Morgan."

Morgan saw the light and hope in her eyes die instantly like a candle being snuffed out. Laura was retreating from him. He frowned. Nervously, she clasped her hands in her lap beneath the table, and he saw her eyes go wary, like a wild animal in a cage. Real terror lapped at the edges of her dark blue gaze.

Grimly, he said, "Near dawn, I woke up from hearing you crying out. At first I thought it was one of my fragmented dreams, because I'd heard your voice in them before. This time," he said heavily, holding her frightened gaze, "it was real."

Laura couldn't stand the suffocating feeling stalking her. She'd had it enough times to realize it was the precursor to an anxiety attack. Abruptly, she stood up, nearly tipping over her chair. Turning, she grabbed it before it could fall on the linoleum floor. She had to do something. Anything! Picking up her plate of uneaten food, she walked to the kitchen sink, her motions robotlike.

Morgan's mouth tightened. He saw pure fear in the depths of Laura's eyes as she walked across to the kitchen. "You don't remember your nightmare?" he asked gently.

"N-no," Laura said, as she placed the plate in the sink. Turning, she came back to the table and picked up the flatware and coffee mug. Though she didn't look at Morgan, she could feel his gaze burning into her. It was a relief to turn back to the sink.

"You were trembling, Laura," Morgan began in a low voice that vibrated with concern. "When I went over to check on you, I touched the shoulder of your gown, and it was wet with sweat."

Hanging her head, the mug poised in her hands over the sink, Laura felt renewed anxiety course through her. "Some nights," she managed to say, "I wake up and find my gown damp." She tried to laugh, but it came out as a choking sound. "It's nothing to be worried about...."

Morgan shook his head. "You were whimpering and moving your head from side to side, as if someone had you pinned, a hand around your throat." He saw her go absolutely still, her lips parting as if in a silent cry. Then a tremor ran through her, as if she'd been physically struck, and the heavy coffee mug slipped from her fingers, shattering into pieces in the sink.

Instantly, Morgan was on his feet, moving swiftly toward her. She was staring in horror at the broken cup, her hands pressed to her lips as she looked down at it. More and more with her, Morgan was discovering he was operating on an instinctive gut level. Settling his hands gently on her rigid shoulders, he felt her tension vibrate through him. He gripped her more tightly, attempting to steady her.

"Laura," he rasped, trying to pull her gently against him. He felt her stiffen, the trembling becoming more pronounced. "Don't fight me," he said, maintaining enough pressure on her shoulders to ask her to let go and trust him—again. Somehow, he knew that Laura always hid her worries from him. Well, this was the wrong time for her to do that. Something so terrifying consumed her that he knew she needed help—his help.

Opening his hands, he spread them flat across her shoulders and, with a light but gentle pressure, continued to ease her back against him. He stifled a groan of pleasure as she surrendered slightly, letting her back, hips and thighs brush against him. "Laura, talk to me—please," he whispered against her ear as her hair tickled his nose and cheek.

Laura quivered in Morgan's grip. How strong he was. Closing her eyes, she felt her terror—all the evil memories—start erupting. He cared. Morgan cared. The same Morgan she loved with quiet desperation was here with her now. The pressure of his hands changed, and she felt herself being turned to face him. Her hands came up automatically to rest against his barrel-like chest. As her palms flattened against his flannel shirt, Laura felt the heavy, slow pounding of his magnificent heart beneath.

His breathing was a solid and steady counterpoint against her quick, ragged breaths.

"Lean on me," he entreated roughly.

Tears burned in her tightly shut eyes as she allowed herself the gift of resting against him. His hands moved in slow circles across her tense shoulders, and with each movement, Laura felt a little more of the tension bleed away.

"That's it," he coaxed thickly, "trust me, Laura. Just trust me. I may not remember a whole hell of a lot, but I do remember feeling some things with you...."

Hope flared sharply within her, and Laura allowed herself to lean a little more heavily against Morgan.

His body was a reassuring presence, shoring up her fragmented state. She felt one of his hands slide around her waist to bring her fully against him. The invisible tie between them was back. She could feel it as surely as she felt each breath he took. How brave he was to step beyond his own wall of pain and suffering to reach out to her. This was the Morgan she knew, the man with the well of endless courage.

"That's better," Morgan whispered, burying his face in her silky hair. "Much better...." And it was. A blazing tenderness moved through him as he held her. He still didn't remember his love for her—at least, in one sense. But in another, he did. Her trembling abated, and he felt her breathing even out, slowing to match his. He felt the rounded softness of her small breasts pressing against his chest, felt the flutter of her smaller heartbeat against his own. She felt so good in his arms. So damn good. He had to remind himself why he was holding her, instead of selfishly absorbing the feel of her to feed his own hungry needs.

"Tell me what happened to you," he ordered thickly. "You've never said anything about your kidnapping. When I've asked Jake or Dr. Parsons, they've gone silent on me. They said I had to get the story from you, Laura." His arms tightened protectively around her slender form. "Well, I'm here, and I'm asking. I want you to tell me what happened."

Shuddering, Laura buried her face deeply in the soft flannel. "Morgan," she whispered unsteadily, "it's nothing compared to what you went through. I—"

He slid his fingers through her hair and held her captive against him. "No, you don't," he muttered. "I'm realizing just how much you avoid, Laura."

She felt his fingers stroking her hair. "I—I suppose I do," she admitted.

He smiled grimly down at her as he eased her away from him just enough to see her suffering features. "No more running," he rasped, "for either of us. Okay? Last night something happened, Laura. I was so scared when I heard you cry out. Something snapped inside me." His gaze probed her tear-filled blue eyes. "I touched your hair, and then something told me to lean down and kiss you."

Her eyes widened.

Morgan's mouth flattened with the admission. "It was selfish of me. I needed you, Laura. Even without memories, I have feelings for you. I did kiss you until you woke up a little. I told you to go back to sleep, and you did." He raised a hand to touch her flaming cheek. "I'm not proud of what I did, but I'm convinced that kiss was the reason I had those dreams and memories. Hell, maybe it was just my worry for you triggering something in my brain. I don't know. It doesn't matter right now. You do." He gave her a small shake. "I want to know what happened to you."

Anguish squeezed Laura's heart. She absorbed the feel of his fingers on her cheek, her skin tingling pleasantly in their wake. The care radiating from him filled her with renewed strength, enough to speak. "I'm so afraid to tell you," she quavered. "I've been dreading this moment for so long, Morgan...."

Her painful words tore at him as nothing he could remember had. Whispering her name, he crushed her hard against him, his hand against the side of her head. "It's all right," he rasped unsteadily. "Whatever it is, Laura, we'll take it together. You hear me? Together.''

The words fell across her, and Laura felt as if she'd crossed the line between sanity and insanity. How many times had she dreamed that Morgan would say those very words to her with just such fervency? With his fierce tenderness aimed at her alone? No, she wasn't going insane—at least, not yet. This was real. She could feel the strength of Morgan's embrace. The powerful beat of his heart gave her courage where she'd had none. Slowly, she eased her hands downward and slid her arms around his waist. She heard Morgan groan—a deep, almost animal-like sound of absolute pleasure.

"I remember waking," she said brokenly, "in this strange house. It was a bedroom. I was sick and dizzy. A guard came into the room when he heard me moving around. I had worn a silk suit because it was our seventh wedding anniversary, and I wasn't in it. Instead, someone had dressed me in a pink silk nightgown. The guard looked at me and left.

"I was very sick, and I sat on the bed looking at my hands. I had rope burns around my wrists, and I kept trying to think how I'd gotten them." Her voice lowered to a broken whisper. "And then ... Garcia came in." She shivered violently and felt Morgan's arms tighten around her in response. Shutting her eyes tightly, Laura said, her voice muffled, "He—he raped me...."

The words escaped, brimming with terror and anguish. Morgan felt tears flood into his eyes. He brushed a kiss against Laura's hair as she began to tremble all over again. A deep longing and tenderness overwhelmed him as he began to rock her gently in his arms. "Let it go," he rasped. "Cry, Laura. Cry. . . ."

A repressed sob jammed Laura's throat. But Morgan's voice was low and husky, and miraculously, the lump dissolved. A cry escaped, tearing violently from her. For an instant, Laura wasn't sure whose sob she'd heard, the sound was so foreign—more animal than human. She felt Morgan's mouth against her temple. He was kissing her, caring for her. Her fingers dug convulsively into his shirtfront, and she struggled to contain the next sob.

"No!" he rasped against her ear. "Let it go! Dammit, Laura, stop trying to run and hide. I'm here. I'll hold you. Just let it go!"

The rawness of his words overran the last remnant of her crumbling defenses. All the months of having to hold herself together—first for Jason, then for herself and finally for the Perseus employees as they frantically tried to locate Morgan—faded away. The last vestiges of her reserve crumbled with a second, tearing sob. Laura buried her face against Morgan's chest and felt his hand in her hair, pressing her face to him. His other arm tightened almost painfully around her waist as he held her as close as possible, as if to absorb her pain into himself.

"Cry for yourself," he growled harshly. "Cry. . ."

And she did. Laura felt her knees give way, felt him take her entire weight as she collapsed against his stalwart frame and gave in to the horror of her experience. One sob after another tore from her contorted mouth. Hot tears, so long held at bay, spilled from her eyes. Her heart felt as if it was exploding with the grief she'd suppressed. Her body convulsed, as the awful, hurting sounds continued rising out of her. Time stood still, losing all meaning as she clutched frantically at Morgan, her hands opening and closing against his shirt as the choking cries rolled up and out of her.

Laura surrendered to her grief—to the hurt she'd sustained from the ordeal—in every way. For this moment out of time, the real Morgan was back. Even if he never regained another memory, she felt him present with her as never before. The invisible connection was strongly anchored between them, more tangible than she'd ever experienced—and it was a lifeline to her in this moment of grief and searing anger.

A deep terror continued to override the rest of her suffering. Even now, as she cried in Morgan's arms, she was afraid to tell him the details of her capture—afraid that if he knew the truth, he'd reject her and want her out of his life—forever. Her body ached from the convulsing sobs, and eventually the storm left her. All she could feel in that moment was Morgan's pounding heart, his hand moving gently across her hair, offering solace. Repeatedly, he placed small kisses along her hairline as he held her close and rocked her gently in his arms.

Where did death end and life begin? Was it possible to feel dead inside, yet still be living? Laura wondered bleakly. Opening her eyes, the remnants of tears clinging to her thick lashes, she stared unseeingly, her cheek pressed firmly against his chest. Her arms ached from holding him so tightly and she let them relax a little. She felt Morgan draw in a deep, ragged breath, felt his warm breath near her ear.

"All right?" he asked huskily.

She nodded jerkily, unwilling to let him go just yet. Morgan must have sensed her fear that he would leave her, because he tightened his embrace momentarily, squeezing her reassuringly.

"That was a long time in coming," he said quietly, easing back just enough to look down at her. Laura's blue eyes were wounded holes of grief. Her lips were still contorted with pain, her velvety cheek damp with tears. He raised a hand to gently dry them. Fresh tears started, and he smiled tenderly, slipping his arm back around her.

"I'm sorry," he said gruffly, "so sorry, Laura. I still don't remember Perseus or what started all this. I can only believe what Jake, Wolf and Killian have told me. But it sounds as if I left you and my family open to attack—"

"No!" Laura pushed away enough to meet his ravaged gaze. "No," she whispered less stridently, "don't blame yourself for what happened, Morgan. It was *no one's* fault. Do you hear me?"

He shook his head. "I should have taken steps to ensure your safety, Laura."

"That's ridiculous!" She pushed back farther, her hands gripping his arms. "Don't you think I knew the risks? I'm part and parcel of the military. I knew when you set up Perseus that someone might seek revenge someday. We talked about the possibility many times, Morgan."

"We did?" He searched her pale features.

"Yes, and we agreed enough precautions had been taken." Laura gestured wearily. "I wasn't willing to live behind iron gates followed by guards. When you suggested it, I said no. If there's any fault here, it's mine.''

Gently, he framed her face, gazing deeply into her injured eyes. "I don't remember those conversations, Laura, but it doesn't matter.''

"I thought,'' she whispered, clinging to his tender gaze, "the worst time in my life was when I was hit by that car and lost my sight. No one knew if I'd recover from the blindness.'' She lowered her lashes. "But this is worse. I—I can't believe what happened to me, sometimes. I have horrible nightmares. I—I was hoping with you near me again, they'd stop.'' Helplessly, she forced herself to look back up into his eyes. "But they haven't.''

"And they shouldn't,'' Morgan said thickly, using his thumbs to wipe the fresh tears from her cheeks. "I just remembered something from the past that I used to tell you.'' He gave her an apologetic look. "I remember telling you how safe you were when you were with me.'' Looking up, suffering deeply, Morgan rasped, "And I didn't keep you safe, Laura. Nor did I keep my family safe. . . .''

Sharp, serrating pain pierced Laura's heart. Laura gripped Morgan's arms tightly. "All we can do,'' she whispered, "is go on. We can't blame ourselves, Morgan. Dr. Parsons said to live one hour at a time— one day at a time. We have to pick up the pieces of ourselves that way. Otherwise—'' she released a ragged sigh "—we'll drive ourselves insane with guilt and pointing fingers. We can't afford to do that. We just can't!''

Hearing the stridency in her voice, he returned his gaze to her. Releasing her, he allowed his hands to settle on her shoulders. "No," he answered heavily, "no finger pointing." Still, Morgan knew without a doubt that this was his fault. Memory or no memory, he'd caused Laura's pain. It was impossible for him to understand yet what the fact of her rape had done to her, but he promised himself he would find out. Though she had cried long and hard, he could see that she looked a little better now; but he could also feel a deeper, more terrifying wound she was still hiding from him. Somehow, he'd regain her trust. And maybe—if he was the luckiest man in the world—he could help her heal the wound he'd caused.

Guilt bubbled within him as he held Laura lightly in his embrace, but a lot of new feelings rose with it. Somehow, that one innocent kiss last night had cracked open the door on his memory—if not specific recollections, then solid feelings he knew were related to his past.

Forcing a partial smile for Laura's benefit, he stroked her hair. "One hour at a time," he promised thickly. "One day at a time."

She managed a grimace. "I'm more worried about the nights. The darkness scares me—" her voice broke "—because that's when Garcia would stalk me...."

"Then we'll handle the nights together, Laura."

Chapter Eight

The sun felt warm and soothing on Laura's back. She had brought one of the folding chairs from the porch of the cabin, along with her needlepoint, to sit along the bank of Oak Creek. In the past seven days the Arizona weather had offered an amazing alternative to the East Coast February she was accustomed to. The temperature was in the high sixties, the sky a blinding blue streaked with long, thin cirrus clouds that reminded her of the soft, downy feathers on a goose's breast.

It was nearly noon, and she languished in the soothing rays while working on an iris design with her needle. One day, it would become a cover for a couch pillow. The work caught and focused her fragmented concentration, and for that she was grateful.

A little farther down the creek's bank stood Morgan, who had borrowed some fly tackle from the Donovan Ranch and was casting endlessly into the cold, flowing water. He'd had no luck yet, but Laura didn't think that mattered much to him. Just getting outdoors, breathing in the clean southwestern air and absorbing the sun's strength was enough.

Morgan. Her heart repeated his name, and her hands stilled over her project. She lifted her chin and watched him. He was at least two hundred feet downstream, dressed in jeans, a blue-and-white flannel shirt, the sleeves rolled carelessly up to his elbows, and hiking boots. The breeze, always present along the creek, lifted errant strands of his black hair.

The tension he'd carried to the cabin seven days ago was gone. His craggy profile had softened. Had it been the miracle that had occurred in the kitchen that first morning after they'd arrived? Laura wondered. Or that kiss she could barely recall, like a hazy strand of fog just out of reach? She wasn't sure. She poked her needle through another hole in the fabric. The week had fled by. Ever since he'd held her in the kitchen and she'd cried out her heart and soul in his arms, those terrible nightmares had ceased stalking her.

In fact, Laura thought as she chose a strand of deep purple thread from the tote bag leaning against the leg of her chair, her sleep had become deep, healing and uninterrupted since then. Six nights of eight hours of sleep had worked miracles on her, too.

As she threaded the purple strand through the needle's eye, she sighed with contentment. Every day, as she watched, small memories came trickling back to Morgan. But so far they were all from his childhood.

How she ached for him to remember *their* time, *their* love. Though they slept only six feet apart, Laura missed Morgan.

Chiding herself for her impatience, she carefully inserted the needle again into the fabric across her lap.

Her heart revolved to Jason and Katy. How she looked forward to calling her children each night. Jason loved the phone and loved to chat. Katy couldn't, of course, but Laura eagerly absorbed Susannah's litany of the children's activities each day. Part of her ached to hold them, to dress them in the morning, tousle Jason's hair and watch the devilish sparkle come to his eyes as she played with him. How like his father he was. And how much Katy was like her....

Morgan had yet to talk to Jason on the phone, and that disturbed Laura. He had no memory of his children and was afraid of raising Jason's hopes. Laura couldn't help but notice how Morgan moved uncomfortably around the cabin as she talked to their family, hidden away in the hills of Kentucky.

What if Morgan's memory was permanently wiped out regarding her and their children? The question was simply too brutal to contemplate. Laura knew she was emotionally unstable and knew it would take months, perhaps a year or more, to get over the shocks she'd suffered. Ann Parsons had dropped by midweek and talked with them individually in her role as therapist. Laura looked forward to talking to Ann, woman-to-woman. There were certain things she simply couldn't share with Morgan yet. Perhaps she never would be able to, if his memory didn't return. Ann provided a cushion, a friendly ear to listen to her worst fears, without judgment or recrimination.

To give Morgan credit, he was trying desperately to jog memories, Laura knew. He often pored over the photo albums she'd brought. They would sit for hours at a time as she slowly and thoroughly went over each color photo with him. Still, he remembered little beyond fragments of his childhood years. Laura knew his parents were grateful he remembered them; Morgan had phoned them as soon as the memories returned and had reestablished contact....

She heard him give a victorious shout and she looked up. He had caught a trout! A smiled played across her lips as she watched him expertly retrieve the fish and place it in the creel at his feet. His face glowed with triumph, and she couldn't resist him any longer. Putting her needlepoint aside, she walked down the bank to join him.

He grinned widely, crouching over his creel as she sauntered up.

"Dinner tonight," he said proudly, gesturing to the shining rainbow trout in the bottom of the basket.

Laura sighed and crouched down opposite him. "He's so big and beautiful, Morgan. It's a shame to see him die." She looked up. "Rachel brought T-bone steaks over yesterday. We could grill them for dinner tonight...."

Crestfallen, Morgan watched the trout flop around in the creel, gasping. "He's big, Laura. A good pound and a half. Do you know how hard it is to catch a trout on a fly rod, much less a big one like this?"

Laughing gently, Laura stood. "Hey, it's your decision. You're the one who spent two hours out here casting for him."

Morgan studied her closely. An ache seized him, and he slowly unwound from his crouched position to stand up. Laura was less than a foot away, wearing a denim skirt that fell to her ankles, a feminine, long-sleeved white blouse and a bright red velvet vest, its crimson color accenting the blush in her cheeks. Hungrily, he absorbed the sparkle in her deep blue eyes as she playfully held his gaze. Her lips were softly parted, and he found himself aching even more to kiss her—again. Each night became more and more of a special hell for him. Laura might fall asleep immediately, as soon as her head hit the pillow, but he sure didn't. No, he lay there fantasizing about touching her, loving her and kissing her senseless.

He didn't question Laura's love for him; it was obvious in so many small ways. Not that she had reached out since that morning in the kitchen to hug him or kiss his cheek—or anything obvious. No, she'd circumspectly kept her distance from him. And he knew it was because he still couldn't recall his love for her. Oh, he had emerging feelings for her, some vague recollections, and he'd shared those with her, but he knew that until he could recall the love they had shared, he couldn't—wouldn't—touch her.

Today her hair was plaited into two braids, the ends tied with red threads from her needlepoint kit. How girlish she looked. He had to fight not to reach out and slide his fingers along the soft slope of her cheek. How badly he needed to touch her again, to bury his face in her thick, blond hair and inhale her special womanly fragrance which made him dizzy with need.

He looked down at the trout, then reached into the creel. In one smooth motion he threw the fish back into the creek.

"Morgan!" Laura cried out in surprise.

He grinned mischievously. "You're next!"

Before she could protest, he swept her up into his arms. With a cry of utter surprise, she threw her arms around his neck. She was wildly aware of his strength. Of him. Laughing, she pressed her face against his neck and jaw as he carried her dangerously close to the churning water.

"You save a trout's life and you pay for it," he told her roughly, grinning down at her. How good she felt against him! She was small and feather light. That familiar fragrance of camellia struck him fully as he stopped near the edge of the bank.

"Morgan! You wouldn't dare throw me in!" Laura gasped. Her eyes grew round as she watched his own gray eyes sparkle with mischief, and she automatically tightened her arms around his massive neck and shoulders. It was the first time Morgan had done anything so spontaneous and she loved it. She loved him.

"Wouldn't I?" he taunted, threatening to swing her out over the stream.

Laughing wildly, Laura gasped, "The old Morgan wouldn't ever do something this dastardly! He saw himself as a white knight come to the rescue!"

"Maybe the new Morgan would," he threatened teasingly. She was so alive, so fresh and innocent in his arms. He absorbed the feel of her body crushed against him. Laura's eyes danced with such joy that he felt his heart opening powerfully beneath her smile. He made a motion as if to toss her into the rushing water. Instantly she shrieked, grabbed him hard and clung to him, her face pressed against his. Morgan couldn't help himself, nor did he want to.

He closed the scant inches between them in an instant, his mouth covering her smiling lips. Instantly, he felt Laura stiffen in his arms with surprise, but just as quickly, she relaxed against him. Something goaded him to continue the kiss rather than draw away as he knew he should. No, he wanted her. Needed her. Relentlessly, he smothered her mouth with his own. Rocking her lips open, he felt how she surrendered to him. Her mouth tasted of sunlight and the honey she'd had on her toast earlier. He felt unmistakable heat and invitation in her returning kiss as her arms tightened around his neck. Her breasts pressed more fully against his chest, and he felt her moan when he ran his tongue across her full lower lip, then recaptured her mouth with even more intensity than before.

His body hardened instantly as he deepened his exploration of her. His breath was coming in ragged gasps, but so was hers. As hungrily as he took her, she gave back equal pressure and heat. How badly he wanted to plunge himself into her molten depths! But something cautioned him not to go that far. Not yet. Instead, he sent his tongue searching her hot, moist mouth. If he'd ever suspected Laura was weak or shy, he'd been mistaken. Her tongue boldly touched and slid along his, and he found himself staggering beneath her equally fierce onslaught. Fire ignited and exploded through him as her tongue danced with his. Moments melted together, and he felt a fusion of their bodies—and their souls.

Her lips were too luscious, and he couldn't get enough of the feel of her soft, surrendering mouth, which continued to tease and beckon him. But gradually, to his dismay, his mind began to work and again take charge, leaving his body hard and aching with need as he reluctantly ended the kiss. Opening his eyes, he gazed stormily into her lustrous ones, half-open and studying him as the sounds of nature returned around them. Her lips glistened in the wake of his kiss, the lower one slightly swollen, and he was instantly sorry for his powerful, unexpected assault upon her.

Morgan gently eased Laura to the ground, his arms still around her shoulders, holding her close. To his joy, she leaned fully against him, her arms encircling his waist. Her unabashed radiance humbled him as nothing else could. Giving her a shaky, apologetic smile, he lifted his hands to smooth back her hair. "I don't know where the hell that came from...."

"I don't care," she whispered, running her palms across his chest, holding his narrowed gray gaze. And she didn't.

"I was..." Morgan scowled and settled his hands back on her small shoulders. "I made a promise to myself not to touch you until I could remember, Laura."

She frowned. "I'm not sorry it happened, Morgan."

"But you remember your love for me."

"Yes...."

Frustration ate at his euphoria. Morgan looked beyond her, his tone gruff. "I don't think it's fair to you—to us—if I kiss you or...whatever...and I don't remember, Laura."

She placed her hands gently on his massive arms. "And what if you don't ever remember us, Morgan?"

His scowl deepened. "I . . . don't know."

"That's what scares me," she whispered unsteadily, trying to smile but not succeeding. "I'll take whatever you want to give me, Morgan. I'm not proud. I love you. I'll always love you, no matter how many of your memories come back—or don't."

He saw the tears glimmering in her eyes. "Don't cry," he rasped, then caught himself. Dr. Parsons had counseled him that crying was often the healthiest thing to do. "Forget I said that."

With a small, choking sound, Laura said, "The old Morgan hated to see me cry, too. Even if you don't remember, you *know,* Morgan."

At the fervency of her voice, he caressed her shoulders tenderly. "I feel as if I'm cheating you—us—if I touch you like this . . . kiss you. . . ."

"Did you lift me up and kiss me just now because you felt you *had* to?" she asked wryly.

He studied her in the silence. A teasing love shone in her eyes. "No," he admitted unsteadily. "It just sort of happened—in the moment. I wasn't thinking about it," he added awkwardly.

Her smile was tender. "One of the things you used to do—quite frequently, as a matter of fact—was steal me from whatever I was doing, lift me into your arms and take me to our secret garden out back."

He raised his eyebrows. "I did?"

Laura touched his recently shaven cheek. "There's a precocious little boy alive and well inside of you, Morgan Trayhern, and I've been privileged to play with him quite often. So lifting me up the way you did, and kissing me..." She smiled. "It was something I not only enjoyed, but could hardly wait to have happen."

"When I would steal you away like that—we'd do more than...kiss?" He caught her hand and pressed his lips to her palm, watching her eyes turn to the dusky blue that told him she was feeling pleasure at his touch.

"Oh..." Laura sighed. "Yes, much more than kissing...."

He had to stop or he was going to lay her down on the green, grassy bank and take her right here and now. Morgan allowed her to reclaim her hand and gave her a crooked smile. "Memories have a funny way of turning up, don't they?"

"Yes, they do." Laura smoothed her skirt across her thighs. "I always loved your spontaneity, Morgan. I thought it was gone, but I was wrong." Her voice grew husky with tears. "And I'm so glad it's back, because it's such a natural part of who you are and how you express yourself...."

Laura snapped awake. What time was it? Slowly she sat up in bed, the covers falling away. Looking to the left, she realized Morgan was gone. She heard another noise. Her heart pounded hard in her chest as she threw her covers off and stood, the floor offering a cold greeting to her bare feet as she retrieved her chenille robe from the end of the bed. What was wrong? Laura groggily sensed something, though she was unable to put a name to it.

Stumbling sleepily from the bedroom, she moved into the living room. A night light illuminated the room enough for her to weave among the furniture and head for the kitchen, where she thought the sounds had emanated from. Pushing hair away from her face, she wondered why Morgan was up. The clock on the shelf read three o'clock.

"Morgan?" she called, her voice thick with remnants of sleep. Halting in the doorway, she saw his shadowy form facing the kitchen sink. He was standing tensely, wearing only his pajama bottoms. His hands gripped the counter, and sweat gleamed on his naked back and shoulders.

Biting her lower lip, Laura felt the charged tension in the kitchen and knew instantly it originated from Morgan. What had happened? A nightmare? He'd had so many over the years, but with time, they'd become less frequent and severe. As she slowly approached him from the side, making sure he could see her, she reached out.

"Morgan?" she whispered, tentatively touching his shoulder. One of the dangers of Post Traumatic Stress Disorder was that, caught up in a flashback, a person might not be grounded in reality, unable to disconnect from the violence of the remembered moment. Laura knew from experience not to come up behind Morgan and throw her arms around him. She could be struck by a fist. Although it had never happened, she'd seen Morgan come close to striking her or whoever was near.

She pressed her fingers more surely against his damp skin. He was trembling, his breathing raspy as he hung his head over the sink, leaning against it for support.

"It's all right, Morgan," she said soothingly, allowing him to feel her hand more fully against his arm. "It's me, Laura. You're safe, Morgan. Safe. You're here, in the cabin with me. Just listen to my voice, and I'll bring you back home.... Listen to me, Morgan."

She moved inches closer, keeping her hand firmly around his upper arm. She knew from experience what would help Morgan when he was trapped by the virulence of his nightmarish past. She kept her voice husky and low, almost singsong, so that he could struggle internally to tear his attention away from whatever was playing out before his tightly shut eyes and transfer his panicked attention to her. In some ways, not much had changed, Laura thought sadly. It grieved her that Morgan was going to continue to have PTSD symptoms. The one blessing of his amnesia had seemed to be that he would mercifully be allowed to forget his Vietnam War days and the loss of his company—and the horror that had haunted him ever since.

Little by little, as she continued speaking quietly to him, his bunched shoulders began to relax. His breathing evened out, and the sweat began to dry on his skin. Where he'd held the edge of the sink in a white-knuckled grip, his hands began to loosen their hold. Gradually, Laura placed her arm around his torso.

"Come on," she entreated gently. "Come and sit down, Morgan. I'll make you some hot tea. Come on, darling...." She chastised herself for allowing the endearment slip from her lips. She'd tried to be so careful in not pressuring Morgan with her love, not wanting to frustrate him more or, worse, drive him away from her. What they had was still so tenuous.

Lifting his head, Morgan turned and stared at Laura. He felt her thin but strong arm around his waist, gently tugging at him to move away from the counter. "I..." His voice came out roughened and hoarse. "Laura, I remember Ramirez... Peru... the whole damned thing...."

A shaft of pain pierced Laura as she stood, holding his ravaged, darkened gaze. "All right," she said unsteadily, "then let's go to the living room, Morgan. You need to talk about it." She guided him out of the kitchen and to the couch. While a part of her was thrilled that a huge chunk of his memory had returned, another part grieved for him because he was being forced to reenter a living hell. As Morgan sat tensely on the couch, his legs spread, his hands clasped between his thighs, she saw the devastation etched on his features.

Biting back a cry, she sat down next to him, her hands resting lightly against his arm and thigh. Such agony showed in his eyes and the slash of his mouth that she wanted to let her own tears flow, but she knew it wouldn't help him. Reaching up, she stroked the dampened hair now clinging to his head. "What happened, Morgan? Tell me what you saw...."

Knotting his hands tightly, Morgan shut his eyes. Just the gentle touch of Laura's hand on his hair broke what little defense was left between him and the memories smashing through him. "I went to sleep," he rasped thickly, staring out across the semidarkened living room. "I was happy as I fell asleep." He twisted his head and held her tender, lustrous gaze. "I was replaying that kiss we shared at the creek today. I felt more whole, stronger than I can remember...."

"That's probably why your mind allowed all these memories to surface," she whispered. "You are getting stronger, Morgan, and Ann warned us that as we regained our emotional health, the traumas would probably be released in ways that we could deal with in a positive fashion." She smiled gently and rested her brow momentarily against his shoulder. "It's a good sign in one way."

"Good, hell," he snarled. "I remember the whole damn sequence, Laura. I remember seeing those sons of bitches entering our bedroom and shooting us with dart-tranquilizer rifles. We were like trapped animals—no warning, no way to protect ourselves."

Her heart pounded briefly in her chest and she stared at his suffering profile. "D-do you remember...us?" Afraid of his answer, Laura felt her throat constrict.

"I'm sorry," he rasped, turning and studying her, "I do remember you in the bedroom with me when we got shot. But I don't remember you or the kids in an emotional sense—yet." He saw the pain in her expression and reached out to grip her hand tightly. "I'm sorry, Laura. All I saw after that was the prison, the torture—"

"No," she said unsteadily, "it's enough, Morgan. More than enough. We shouldn't be talking about that, anyway. Talk to me about what you do remember...."

It was dawn by the time Morgan finished recounting his horrifying months in Ramirez's fortress. He felt weakened emotionally from reliving those tortured days. At the same time he experienced a killing rage toward the man who had taken so much away from him. As he'd talked, he'd sat facing Laura, holding her small, warm hands while he grew chilled and tense. Something healing rose out of talking to Laura about his experience. As the pictures and feelings flowed out of him, Morgan saw the anguish in her eyes, in the way her lips parted—for him and what he'd endured.

"I know there's more," he told her harshly at last. "I feel it here, in my gut."

Laura nodded and whispered unsteadily, "I'm sure there is, but your mind has given you plenty to assimilate and work through for now, Morgan. More than enough."

Staring down at her hands, he said, "You're so small, yet so damned strong. You amaze me, Laura. You always have...." He had no idea where those words had come from. But he knew now that when things like that came out of him without forethought, it was the old, deep knowing surfacing. He saw her eyes grow warm, shining with unspoken love.

"I wish," he said huskily, "that of all the memories coming back, I'd remember you. Our love..."

"I know," she said quietly, "but in one sense, it will probably be the last thing you'll remember, Morgan."

"Why?"

"Because our love wasn't traumatic to you. Ann has told me many times that your mind and body will work together to rid you first of what can hurt you or perhaps turn into a health problem. The love we had was the healthiest aspect in you and in me." She shrugged painfully. "So we wait."

"It's hurting you," he muttered, watching as she avoided his sharpened gaze. "I see it in a hundred small ways every day, Laura."

She eased her hands from his. Her mouth curved into a bittersweet smile. "I know...but it's all right, Morgan. Really, it is. It's not your fault. I know you're trying to remember."

Hanging his head, he pushed his fingers through his hair. "In some ways, I wonder if I'm not hurting you more by being here with you, Laura."

"No!" The word came out filled with anguish—and terror.

Morgan stared at her, seeing her face go pale. "I didn't mean I'd leave," he said quickly, reading her gaze. "I'm not leaving, Laura."

Pressing her hand to her pounding heart, she hung her head. "We're in a catch-22, Morgan. If you walked away and left me, I don't know if I could make it. I hate admitting that to you—or to myself. I've always prided myself on being able to stand on my own two feet, to handle whatever life threw at me." She closed her eyes tightly and her voice became scratchy. "But right now, I'm feeling horribly vulnerable and weak. I'm not as strong as you may think...and I hate myself for feeling that way. I've never had to lean on you...."

Sliding his hand along her clean jawline, Morgan gently made her look at him. "It's always been the other way around, hasn't it, Laura? Because of my past, the PTSD, I've needed you, needed to lean on you and use the resources you've always given me without a thought?"

It hurt Laura to look at the tender, burning light in his eyes. "Y-yes," she whispered painfully. "I never minded, Morgan. Never. I love you, and that's part of loving a person—being there to help them through whatever hell they're going through."

"But it's different this time, isn't it? Something bad happened to both of us. I guess I'm used to leaning on you, using you, but this time it cuts both ways. We don't have a past track record in our marriage for handling this, so I guess we're both floundering a little within ourselves and with each other."

He was right, and for some reason, Laura felt ashamed of herself, of her inability to be as strong as she always had been before. "I'm sorry, Morgan—"

With a shake of his head, he rasped, "Don't ever be sorry, Laura." His hand stilled against her cheek. "I may not remember my love for you, or all the times we've shared, but my heart tells me marriage is a two-way street. Aren't there times when one partner leans and the other supports, and vice versa?"

The rough gentleness of his voice tore at Laura, and she closed her eyes and choked back a sob. "Y-yes..."

"Then lean on me when you feel like it."

She sniffed and opened her eyes. "Morgan, you're already over the top with your own stuff. I'm not about to add mine to it. You're strong, I know that. But even you have your limits."

His smile was very male and very caring as he studied her in the gray light of dawn filtering through the living room windows. "Let me be the judge of that, Laura."

"Our marriage never worked that way," she argued weakly.

"Then," he said, pushing several tendrils of hair away from her temple, "it's about time for our marriage to change."

Chapter Nine

Shortly after he'd finished talking to her about his Peruvian prison memories, Morgan had taken a hot shower and gone back to bed. Laura had remained up, too tense and shaken by their conversation to fall asleep. She tried needlepoint, but her hands trembled too much, and her concentration kept ranging back over Morgan's three months at Ramirez's hands.

When the dawn turned to daylight, she changed from her nightgown and robe into a heavy, rainbow-colored sweater, Levi's and hiking boots. She found a sheepskin coat in the closet, and though it was too big for her, she shrugged it on and left the cabin.

The walk along the bank of Oak Creek, its yellowed grass interspersed with fresh shoots of green, all thickly coated with frost, helped clear her mind and emotions—to a degree. Her hands tucked in the fleece-lined pockets, Laura watched a bald eagle wing silently down the creek, looking for a fish for its breakfast. The appearance of the dark brown fishing eagle with its brilliant white head and tail shook her out of her own lingering sadness for a moment.

Then she looked up and saw a second eagle circling a little higher in the sky. She stood on the bank, her neck craned, realizing vaguely that bald eagles mated for life. In some ways she was like that loyal eagle, she realized—it would take death to separate her from Morgan. Well, that had almost happened, she thought glumly. Her heart had actually stopped beating on the deck of that Coast Guard helicopter, though she didn't remember much of the actual event, except that she'd been surrounded by brilliant white light. When she'd regained consciousness, Noah, Morgan's brother, had been leaning over her, gripping her hand, looking at her worriedly.

Why couldn't she feel happy about Morgan's returning memory? Laura kicked herself mentally for being selfish. She should be happy for him, regardless of what piece of memory it was that came to him. Resolving to try to find the strength somewhere within her to remain Morgan's staunch guiding light, she returned to the cabin.

"What time is it?" Morgan asked thickly as he moved slowly out of the bedroom, rubbing his face tiredly.

Laura swallowed hard. "It's noon." Morgan wore only blue-and-white-striped pajama bottoms, and they outlined his magnificent lower body to perfection. As he stood in the living room doorway, looking at her where she sat near the warmth of the wood stove, she savored his drowsy state. He had put on at least ten pounds in the week they'd been at the cabin. He was eating like the proverbial workhorse, and his once-pronounced ribs were fleshed out again, his barrel chest covered with black hair—a chest she'd slid her hands provocatively across so many times before. An ache centered deep in her womb, and she knew she wanted to physically love Morgan. Her mind whispered that it was impossible right now, and she felt the bitter blade of truth cutting into her heart again.

Morgan dropped his hands from his face and hungrily absorbed the vision of Laura's slight form. He thought she looked beautiful in the colorful sweater, which hung halfway down her long, curved thighs. Her hands were clasped in front of her as she sat a few feet from the stove, warming herself. Sunshine lanced through the southern windows, and Morgan noticed a sheepskin coat on the couch. He moved toward her and instantly saw her face change. Or did he?

Still groggy from his exhausted sleep, he moved to within inches of her, facing the fire and holding his own hands toward it. Laura got up and moved away from him until a few feet separated them. "Did you crash on the couch here after I went back to bed?" he asked.

Laura shook her head. "No... I was too upset by what you shared with me. As soon as it got light, I took a long walk down by the creek."

"That explains the coat," he muttered.

"Oh... yes." Morgan didn't miss much, but then, he never had. Nervously, she sat down again on one of the chairs, crossing her legs and folding her hands in her lap. Being this close to Morgan was torture of another type. He was so tall and male—and she ached to touch him, to memorize his body with her hands and lips. To explore him leisurely with love.

"Did you see my trout?" he asked, a grin edging his mouth. He rubbed his face, feeling the bristles of his beard. He needed to shave.

Laura laughed faintly. "No, I didn't see him, but I saw two beautiful bald eagles flying up the canyon, looking for breakfast."

"Eagles?" Morgan raised his eyebrows. "I didn't know Arizona had bald eagles."

She shrugged delicately. "Well, unless I've completely flipped out, I saw them." She managed a half laugh. "Maybe I was hallucinating. Anymore, I have a tough time distinguishing reality from...everything else."

Morgan felt his heart squeeze in response to her whispered words. He saw the translucence of her features, saw her delicate beauty and her fragile, vulnerable state. Right now he felt more solid, more sure of himself than she did, he realized. But then, she had been the first to be rescued—had gone through two grueling months alone, wondering if he was alive or dead. She'd taken a more brutal daily beating than he had, in many ways.

Scowling, he draped his hands on his narrow hips and studied the sun-splashed pine floor, shining golden beneath his feet. "Let's do something together today," he began in a low voice. "Something different. Fun."

"What?"

Morgan lifted his head and studied her in the gathering silence that stretched between them. He saw hope suddenly spring to life in her eyes and in the way her lips parted. He'd kissed those beautiful, full lips. He'd tasted Laura's passion, and he wanted a hell of a lot more of it. Tearing his thoughts from his own naked needs, he said, "Remember, Rachel told us about a pretty spot about two miles up Oak Creek? She said it was a nice area for a picnic." He twisted his head and looked out the window. "Looks to me like a nice enough day—blue skies and sunshine." Settling his gaze back on her, he said, "How about it? Are you up to fixing us a picnic lunch? I'll find a blanket, make some coffee, and we'll spend part of the afternoon exploring that area."

"Yes—I'd like that, Morgan."

"We need a break," he muttered, running his fingers through his hair. "We've gone through a lot in such a short amount of time. I'd like to change the pattern and let nature take our attention for a while."

Laura nodded. "It sounds wonderful, Morgan. Let's do it."

His grin was uneven but boyish. "Together..."

Laura tried to hide her awe of the place Rachel Donovan called "the pond." It wasn't actually a pond, but rather a place where Oak Creek spilled into a widened area perhaps two hundred feet in diameter. There the rushing water became as smooth and glassy as a lake before narrowing to a bottleneck at the other end and once again becoming a tumbling, rushing creek. The bank where they stood was rocky; on the other side rose a red sandstone cliff capped with a black lava layer a hundred feet thick.

The cliff stood a good two thousand feet high. Trees, most of them smooth, white-barked sycamores interspersed with aspens and evergreens, crowded the water's banks. Luckily, Morgan was good at following the infrequently used trail that paralleled the creek, and they'd managed to discover the beautiful spot.

He stood on the bank now, appreciating the dark, clear pool of water before them. He'd put on a light blue chambray shirt and tan chinos with his leather hiking boots for the day. He turned and smiled as Laura joined him. "Pretty spot, isn't it?"

"Yes," she whispered. "When I think of Arizona, I think of desert, not a mountainous spot like this."

"Reminds me more of Montana's trout creeks high in the Rockies," he murmured, agreeing with her.

"You did a lot of hunting and fishing with your father, growing up, as your family moved from one Air Force base to another," Laura told him.

Scratching his head, he said, "I don't remember much about that, but I feel it." The breeze was warm and intermittent. As Morgan studied Laura, whose face was flushed from hiking at the six-thousand foot altitude, he smiled. For some reason, she'd left her hair loose and free—the way he liked it—instead of capturing it in a ponytail or braids today. Sunlight danced across her crown, creating a halolike effect.

Reaching out, he gently grazed her hair. "You look like my guardian angel at this moment," he whispered thickly. Allowing his hand to fall back to his side, he saw the surprise in her expression as she turned to look up at him. "Inside me—" he tapped his chest where his heart lay "—I know you've always been an angel looking out for me, haven't you?"

Laughing and embarrassed, Laura turned and took the red plaid blanket and, with his help, laid it out on the creek bank in the sunshine. "Angel? Oh, I don't know, Morgan. I may look like an angel to you, but believe me, I can fall off that pedestal pretty quickly. I have my days," she warned with a smile.

Morgan eased the pack off his back. He'd already rolled up his sleeves. "I can't imagine that even on your worst day you're really all that bad," he teased back. He began taking the food and the thermos of coffee from the knapsack and arranging them on the blanket. The temperature was in the high fifties and the sun made it seem even warmer. He hadn't worn a coat. Though Laura had, she'd shed it halfway to this spot of heaven on earth, because hiking at the high altitude, on a slow, continual upgrade, was enough to heat up anyone.

Settling on the blanket, her legs tucked beneath her, Laura sorted through the bacon-lettuce-and-tomato sandwiches. Morgan sat less than a foot away, legs crossed, a contentment she'd not seen since his kidnapping visible on his features.

"I'm not all sweetness and light," she warned again.

"What were you like on your bad days?" he wondered, slowly unwrapping one of the thick sandwiches.

Laura opened the thermos and poured them each a cup of steaming, black coffee. "I could get in snits, Morgan."

"Over what?" he asked, munching on the salty, tasty fare. He enjoyed watching every movement

Laura made. She had such inborn grace, it was like watching a ballerina dance. When he realized she wasn't going to eat, he unwrapped another sandwich and handed it to her. She reluctantly took it, after setting her coffee aside.

"Well?" he prodded amiably, "what would set you off? More than likely, I imagine it was something I did or didn't do. Right?" He kept his tone light and teasing, sensing that was what she needed right now.

Laura held the sandwich and looked toward the pool, dancing with sparkles of sunlight. The sky above them was such an intense, deep blue that it took her breath away, and the persistent sun warmed her inner coldness. With birds providing a private symphony around them, the spot was, indeed, heaven on earth, as Rachel had promised. Laura wished she could truly absorb the peace and solitude that surrounded them, instead of feeling like a torn-up battlefield inside.

"Laura?"

At the sound of Morgan's deep, thoughtful voice, she roused herself. "Sorry," she murmured.

"Why don't you eat a little something?" He gestured to the sandwich in her hands. "Come on, at least half?"

Making a face, she bit into the sandwich and chewed, though it tasted like cardboard to her. Laughing inwardly, she admitted to herself that her five senses had been horribly skewed by the rapes. Not wanting to dwell on those thoughts, she forced herself to swallow, the food becoming a lump in her throat. She reached for the coffee and took several sips.

"Look," Morgan said, pointing across the shallow expanse of the pond, "there's a deer path or something going up that cliff face."

Peering in the direction he was pointing, Laura saw a small, thin path that appeared frequently. "Yes, I see it now." She smiled at him. "You're more eagle than you realize."

"The deer must come off the top of that wooded rim." He gestured to the lava crown, thickly forested with pine trees, that topped the cliff. "They probably come down at dawn and dusk, to drink and feed."

Responding to his enthusiasm, Laura said, "Why don't we go over there after lunch and look for prints in the sand? I'll bet you can tell me what animals come down to drink." She wanted desperately to turn the spotlight on Morgan, not herself.

He studied her intently for a moment, watching a blush cover her cheeks as she purposely avoided his stare. Sensing her internal panic, he'd backed off from making her reveal parts of herself. Morgan was a little amazed he could feel her emotions so clearly. Had he always? He wanted to ask, but decided against it. Damn his hungry need to know everything about Laura. He was pushing her, and it was the last thing she needed right now.

"Okay," he murmured, "after you eat your sandwich, we'll find a place to cross above this pond. We'll go over there and test what I think I've forgotten."

"I'd like that." Relief flowed through Laura and she bowed her head, forcing herself to eat the sandwich. She knew Morgan would give her grief if she didn't eat, and she wanted to avoid any kind of confrontation today. Instead, she wanted to pretend their awful past hadn't happened—that they were simply enjoying the day and each other—as they would have before the kidnapping.

"Look at this," Morgan said as he crouched on the bank. "I see raccoon, skunk and deer tracks."

Laura knelt nearby in the thin ribbon of sand along the bank. Everywhere else, pebbles, rocks and boulders followed the twisting, winding creek. They had found a place above the neck of the pool to cross, and her fingers still tingled where Morgan had gripped her hand to help her safely across the wet, slippery stones to the other side.

"What about here?" she said, noticing another, much larger print.

Frowning, Morgan moved around her and in the direction she pointed. "I'll be damned," he whispered, lightly touching the imprint in the sand.

"What?"

"If I'm not mistaken, that's a cougar print."

"You're kidding!"

He shook his head, looking around for more. "No, I'm not. I'm glad we're here together. If this cat was hungry and there was only one of us, he might think he'd found lunch the easy way."

Laura laughed lightly and stood. "He'd take one look at me and think I was far too skinny for a meal."

Morgan grinned and rose to his own full height. In that moment, Laura looked blindingly beautiful to him. The wind had tousled her hair to frame her flushed features, and her dark blue eyes sparkled. Unable to help himself, he walked over and held her face between his palms. Looking deeply into her widening eyes, he said thickly, "You know, I was worried at first when I didn't recognize you, Laura. I remember drawing a blank when you told me your name and that you were my wife." His fingers tightened almost imperceptibly. "But the more I'm around you, the more I share time and space with you, it really doesn't matter anymore to me."

Laura closed her eyes and absorbed his quiet strength, the unexpected touch of his hands upon her, feeling guilty of being so greedy for him. "Wh-what do you mean, Morgan?" she whispered, her hands coming to rest on his arms.

He smiled tenderly. "I mean that even if we don't have a remembered past with each other, it doesn't matter anymore to me." Taking a ragged breath, he murmured, "If today was the first day I'd ever seen you, I know I would learn to care for you...."

Laura opened her eyes, and studied him in the lulling silence. Had she heard correctly? Or, like so many other times, was this some desperate fabrication of her overworked imagination? Morgan had said he cared—about her. She blinked, assimilating his words. He'd not used the word *love*—in reality, he couldn't. He'd only known her three weeks, according to his mind, which refused to divulge their rich, wonderful past together.

It didn't matter to Laura. She was so emotionally unstable that she would take anything Morgan could give her. Right now, she needed him more than he needed her. Perhaps Dr. Parsons was right: once she felt safe, with Morgan back in her life, she would slowly begin to release all the trauma and pressure she'd endured. Ann had warned her she would have a "letdown," and that it could make her feel highly volatile and unstable. She realized she hadn't fully understood the warning—until now.

Still, Morgan's words gave her a badly needed sense of hope in the out-of-control world that was flying apart within her, and Laura was wildly aware of his roughened, scarred hands cupping her face. Her lips parted, and in those moments, she saw the change in his penetrating gray eyes, felt the shift of energy around them. Morgan was going to kiss her. And she wanted to feel his kiss again.

Leaning up on tiptoe, Laura wound her arms around his neck, straining to meet and touch his descending mouth. Nothing had ever seemed so right. Morgan could learn to care for her all over again— whether his memories of them ever returned or not. She would settle for this new caring. But as his lips brushed her, a tiny voice in the back of her head asked her if he was saying these things to ease her anxiety. The old Morgan would never have done that, but Laura had already seen some new, surprising facets to Morgan, completely unlike the man she'd known. Who was the real one? What was important to him now? Was he capable of lying to her to make her feel better?

The thoughts nipped viciously at her as she felt his groan, his mouth plundering hers with fiery intensity. Laura shoved the nagging ideas aside, melting beneath the onslaught of his powerful mouth. She felt the sandpaper quality of his cheek against hers, felt the explosion of moist breath he released as he took her. Her breasts were pressed against his chest, her hips covered by his large hand drawing her insistently against him. Need flowed through her as her pelvis met and melded solidly with his. He felt so strong and good to her, transforming every square inch of her into a caldron of throbbing heat.

She ached to undress him and allow her hands to slide beneath the flannel of his shirt, range across his hairy chest, feeling his muscles tighten beneath her assault. His mouth was searching, and she allowed him deeper entry. Vaguely, she was aware of the hand that had imprisoned her hips moving upward across her sweater to cup her breast.

Her skin pulsed with desire as he caressed her, and she moaned against his mouth. Beyond thinking, she turned, allowing him better access to her yearning breast. If only...oh, if only he would touch her more! His mouth took hers expertly, completely, and she spiraled into the heart of the fire.

A gunshot rang out, echoing through the canyon.

Morgan tore his mouth from Laura's and turned toward the sound of the shot. His arms moved protectively around her, pressing her completely against him, his body a shield. His heart was pounding, his breathing quick as he anxiously searched the surrounding forest. Where had that shot come from? A hunter? Was it Major Houston shooting at a professional hit man sent to hunt them? A hundred thoughts jammed Morgan's mind.

Vaguely he heard Laura gasp, and felt her go on guard, twisting in his arms.

"No," he ordered roughly, remaining positioned between her and the direction from which the shot had come.

"Who's firing?" Laura cried, gripping his arms, her gaze flying from his stony expression to the area across the creek where the shot seemed to have originated.

"I don't know," Morgan answered roughly, suddenly turning and dragging her with him. "Let's go...."

Laura moved quickly as Morgan guided her up the rocky deer trail, which wound steeply upward among the massive, red-sandstone spires. Before too long, Morgan stopped, maneuvering her so that she was fully protected by rock, and surveyed the woods below.

Trying to control her breathing, Laura pressed her hand against her pounding heart. The kiss they'd shared had been incredibly beautiful, freeing. And now, a gunshot. Keeping her voice low, she placed a hand on Morgan's tense shoulder and asked, "Could it be a hunter?"

"In February? I don't know of any hunting season this time of year."

Laura bit down on her lower lip, which was still throbbing with the memory of Morgan's mouth. "A hit man?" She hated to say it. Hated to admit that even here the damnable drug ring could invade, shattering the pieces of their lives they were so desperately trying to fit back together. She felt a white-hot rage at the intrusion.

"It's possible," Morgan growled, frowning as his gaze continued to range across the wooded area. "I don't see anything."

"The shot sounded a long way off...."

"Yes," he grunted, "it did."

"This is a canyon. Sound carries." Laura gulped, her heart beginning to steady a little. No more shots had rung out. "Do you think Mike is on top of it?"

"It could've been Houston in the first place," Morgan said, easing into a crouched position and continuing to watch. "He might have been making his rounds and run into someone."

Shivering, Laura stepped back and wrapped her arms around herself. "Oh, God, Morgan, I thought this was over and done with."

He twisted to look up at her. "It could be nothing," he warned her more gently. The paleness of Laura's features struck him, and he unwound and turned, putting his arms around her. She was trembling like a frightened animal. "Don't jump to conclusions," he said thickly, sweeping her close and holding her tightly. Little by little, he felt Laura's tension dissolve. Kissing her hair and her temple, he divided his attention, his hearing still keyed to the forest below them.

He wondered if it could have been one of Garcia's hit men who had found them. Maybe Houston had intercepted him. Morgan scowled and held Laura firm. Just when they were getting somewhere, just when it seemed they could put their nightmare behind them, their fragile new world had been shattered with a single shot. Damn! The effect on Laura was startling—and frightening. Her blue eyes had turned nearly black, her pupils huge with terror. Her flushed, fair complexion had gone translucent, the skin appearing to stretch across her cheekbones.

"We'll stay here for about half an hour, then we'll take another route back to the cabin," he told her brusquely. "We won't retrace our steps, just in case...."

"And then?" Laura asked, her voice muffled against his chest as she continued to cling tightly to him. "What then?"

"We'll make sure the cabin is safe—then I'll go inside and call the main ranch. Maybe they can tell us what happened."

Squeezing her eyes shut, Laura nodded. She buried her face against him, needing the security of his arms around her. Right now, she felt nakedly vulnerable. The gunshot had stripped her of any pretense of safety. Terror sizzled through her, and it was all she could do to hang on to her sanity. Would their lives ever know peace again?

Chapter Ten

Laura sat huddled on the sofa, her gaze riveted on Major Mike Houston as he grimly entered the cabin. Morgan stood near the couch, his hand resting lightly on her shoulder. Somehow, he seemed to know how badly she needed his continued contact. Inside, she was quivering.

If it hadn't been for Morgan's cool, clear thinking, Laura knew she would have become hysterical. But after making it back to the cabin and finding it empty, Morgan had made a phone call to the ranch, contacting Rachel Donovan. She, in turn, had contacted Mike via portable radio, and he'd promised to drive over and tell them what he'd discovered.

Judging by the grim set of the major's mouth, Laura expected the worst. The Army officer was dressed in gray-and-black tiger fatigues, a pistol riding low on his hip as he walked through the doorway and took off his cap.

"Helluva thing," he said in greeting as he came to a halt just inside the living room. "Someone, a local, was deer hunting."

"Deer hunting?" Laura whispered, looking up at Morgan's fierce countenance.

Mike grinned sheepishly. "That's all it was, so you can both relax. He was hunting out of season and without a license."

"You caught the guy?"

"Yes, I did. The Coconino County sheriff is coming out to pick him up at the ranch." Mike relaxed a little and waved his hand. "You knew the three Donovan daughters run the ranch, didn't you?"

Laura shook her head. "I knew their parents died, but I thought it was only Rachel running the ranch."

"Yes, their parents died in a senseless car crash—a drunk driver hit them head-on. Anyway, the three daughters have all come home from the various parts of the country where they were living. When Rachel heard the gunshot, I was patrolling the area along the creek, and I got lucky. I was probably about a quarter of a mile from the shooter. Rachel thought it was her sister, Kate, who—" he frowned and his voice lowered slightly "—just got out of prison and—"

"Prison?" Morgan demanded tightly. "What was she in for?"

Laura shivered and wrapped her arms more tightly around herself.

Mike held up his hand. "Kate was in prison for three years at a federal facility near Phoenix. She was put there for conspiring to blow up a nuclear power plant. She's an eco-terrorist. Anyway, Rachel thought it was Kate shooting." Shrugging, Mike said, "She called me to say it was probably Kate causing trouble for them—again. It didn't ring true with me because Kate doesn't believe in killing animals, but right now there's a lot of tension at the ranch. Rachel and Jesse are the two younger daughters. They were running things on their own until Kate got out of prison last week."

Morgan scowled. "But it wasn't Kate?"

"No, just a kid about eighteen, trying his luck—out of season." Mike looked at them in the gathering silence. "Are you all right?"

With a sigh, Morgan nodded. "Just spooked, is all."

"Laura?"

"A little hysterical," she jested weakly. "Mike, are we safe with Kate Donovan around? Aren't eco-terrorists fanatical and dangerous?"

"I only met her yesterday," he admitted. "But no, Laura, from what little I got out of her about her prison time, she doesn't strike me as dangerous." He shrugged. "I'll ask Ann—I mean, Dr. Parsons—to keep an eye on Kate since I can't be in two places at once. My main focus is patrolling the area around your cabin, but Dr. Parsons is in constant touch with me via radio, and I'm sure she'll apprise me of anything unusual. As it looks now, Kate's return to the family fold has really put an edge on the two younger daughters."

"How?" Laura asked, slowly unwinding from her position. Maybe if she got up and moved around, she'd feel less helpless and frightened.

"Let's put it this way: Rachel and Jesse don't exactly get along with Kate. It's obvious they don't share her feelings about eco-terrorism, and they're ashamed of her having been in prison. There's no open hostility, but I gotta tell you, you can cut the air with a knife when those three women are in the ranch house together."

"Mike, would you like a fresh cup of coffee?" Laura asked, pausing at the kitchen doorway. She had to do something to bleed off her nervousness.

He nodded gratefully. "That would be great, Laura. But look, you don't need to put yourself out—"

"I want to do it," she said with a slight smile. "Why don't you come in and relax for a while? How about if you and Morgan sit and talk out here at the kitchen table?"

"Sure," Houston said.

Morgan smiled. "Coffee sounds good, Laura. Thanks."

Laura pulled the coffee can down from the cabinet and put some of the fragrant grounds into the dispenser, part of her tension dissolving under the familiar motions. Her hands trembled, but she ignored them.

"So, how are you getting along at the ranch with Dr. Parsons?" Morgan asked Mike.

Mike flushed and grinned. "It's not exactly tough duty, if you want the truth."

Scratching his head, Morgan said, "I don't have any memory of Ann from before yet, but from what I can see of her now, she's very special."

"You picked a winner when you hired her for Perseus," Mike agreed. "Frankly, since Kate has come home, I'm glad she's at the ranch. The other two women were so uptight about their sister's return that if Ann hadn't corralled them separately and let them talk out their fears, things could have been a lot more rocky than they are right now.''

"Pretty tentative?" Laura asked, twisting to look across her shoulder as she flipped on the coffeemaker's switch.

"Ann says Rachel and Jesse are more ashamed of their older sister than anything. But from what I've seen of Kate, she doesn't strike me as a violent person."

"So," Laura said, placing some sugar cookies she'd made a few days earlier on the table, "you don't think she's a problem for us?"

Mike eagerly took a cookie, giving her another grateful look. "Ann...er, Dr. Parsons and I didn't even know about Kate or the situation until she showed up yesterday on the ranch house doorstep. Rachel and Jesse never mentioned her to us. We think they were hoping she would go somewhere other than 'home' after her release. But Kate doesn't seem the terrorist type." He frowned and munched on the cookie. "Matter of fact, she's real quiet and doesn't say much at all."

Rubbing his jaw, Morgan said, "I finally got my memory back from the time spent with Ramirez in the jungle. That was prison to me."

Houston gave him a sympathetic look. "That wasn't prison, Morgan, that was hell. There's a difference."

"The point I'm making," Morgan said, "is that Kate's been behind bars for three years."

"Yes, she was at a maximum-security women's prison, which meant she was behind bars, with only one hour a day to walk the yard and get a little fresh air and sunshine."

Laura shook her head. "I can't imagine that. I'd go insane."

"That's why I don't think Kate is going to be a problem," Houston said. "She's spending most of her times outdoors and with the horses, riding and staying out in nature. Usually, she only comes in to eat and sleep."

"Terrorists don't usually operate alone," Morgan murmured. "Do you think some of Kate's buddies will come around now that she's out?"

"I don't know, but it's something I'm looking into. I've got Sean Killian from Perseus working on that angle. He's getting Kate's record from the feds. By the time I get back to the ranch this afternoon, there ought to be a sizable packet of information waiting for me to look through."

Laura poured fresh coffee into mugs and handed them to the men, who murmured their thanks. Pouring a third cup for herself, she sat down with them.

"What if Kate does have terrorist friends who aren't in prison?"

"There's a chance they could come to the ranch, I suppose," Mike said, sipping the coffee with relish. "This is damn, er, darn good coffee, Laura."

She smiled gently. "Thanks." Mike Houston was a typical old school military man, she thought. She liked his rugged square face, and alert eyes. In some ways, he was like Morgan, but he had an easygoing, relaxed quality that Morgan didn't possess. Maybe Morgan had been like that at one time, in his days as an eager young Marine Corps officer. If so, it had been destroyed with so much else on that hill in Vietnam.

"Oh," Mike said, giving them a look of apology, "I meant to tell you that Customs in Miami picked up one of Garcia's hit men trying to make it into the States. We believe he was one of two men sent to kill you."

Laura's hands tightened around the white mug. She frowned and looked at Morgan, whose gaze narrowed thoughtfully over the information. "What about the other one?"

"They're still looking for him."

"Even if they catch him, there's no guarantee we're safe," Morgan told her. "Garcia could have sent a dozen other men we don't know about."

"I—I know," Laura said faintly. She opened her cold hands briefly. "I just wish this was over. All of it. I wish we could put our lives back together and have a sense of security again, that's all."

Morgan glanced at Houston and back to Laura. He could see the devastation the gunshot scare had wrought. Although it had shaken him up, too, he wasn't traumatized by it as Laura was. "I think Mike will agree with me on this," he told her gruffly. "Once your sense of safety has been compromised, it never truly comes back, Laura. At least, not like before."

Houston finished his coffee. "Unfortunately, you're right," he agreed. "Listen, I gotta saddle up." He grabbed a handful of cookies, nodded deferentially to Laura and stood. "I'll be in touch if there's anything in Kate Donovan's file that I think you'll be interested in knowing."

"Fine," Morgan said, also rising. He saw how tense Laura had become and felt helpless to offer her the safe harbor she longed for. "Come on, Mike, I'll walk you to your vehicle."

Laura pulled herself slowly out of sleep. What had awakened her? She keyed her hearing to Morgan. A week had passed since the rifle incident, and he'd slept soundly every night. Maybe it wasn't him at all that had awakened her. Drowsily, she went over the possibilities. Kate Donovan, according to Mike Houston, wasn't a threat to them. Garcia's second hit man was still on the loose—somewhere. Mike was continuing his patrols. What had awakened her?

A silent alarm was screaming inside her head. The cabin was cool, her blankets drawn cozily around her shoulders. Somehow the gunshot incident seemed to have released a pressure valve within Morgan: he'd been more relaxed since then. But Laura wasn't so lucky, often awakening around three o'clock. She would quietly get up, make some tea and sit in the living room, thumbing through a magazine or something until she felt the fear ebb enough for her to return to her bed and go back to sleep.

As she lay now, keying her hearing to outside noises around the cabin, she caught the far-off hoot of a great horned owl. The rush and bubble of Oak Creek was always soothing, and she loved the sound of it. No, she could hear nothing out of place. Her focus moved back to Morgan. In the past seven days he'd not touched her. That wonderfully melting kiss they'd so hungrily shared by the pool had been the last attempt at intimacy between them.

Closing her eyes, Laura sighed, her hands tightening around her pillow. How many times had she seen that hungry look in Morgan's eyes? Yet, he'd never tried to touch or kiss her again. She could see him seesawing between wanting her and holding himself in iron control. Morgan was a man of principles and integrity, and Laura knew he was wrestling with the devil himself because he'd told her he wouldn't make love to her until he could remember their shared past. He'd said it wasn't fair to her, and he was right. At the same time, Laura thought wearily, feeling the fingers of sleep tugging at her, she needed Morgan's touch, his embrace. Had she communicated that to him? No.

Every day since that gunshot had broken their idyll had been a special hell on earth for her. Gradually, over the past week, Laura realized why. The sound had aroused a blocked memory of her own; Garcia had had one of his guards shot to death in front of her when she was a prisoner at Plantation Paloma. The drug lord had dragged her, dressed in her nightgown, out of her bedroom prison, had hauled her downstairs and behind the huge house and made her watch the man shot by a firing squad. The young soldier's only mistake had been showing up half an hour late for guard duty on the second floor where her bedroom was located.

Laura hadn't known anything about the situation. Her door was always kept locked, and even though she tried to find a way to escape, the windows had had heavy bars across them. She'd had no idea the guards, on duty twenty-four hours a day outside her door, had left her alone for a short time. But when she'd been dragged into the yard, she'd seen the abject terror in the soldier's brown eyes. When she'd tried to cover her face with her hands to avoid seeing him shot, Garcia had yanked them down forcing her to watch the execution.

After trying for a long time to work through those awful memories, Laura felt herself begin to spiral back into sleep. Just as she sighed and surrendered to the process, she heard Morgan scream.

She sat straight up in bed, the covers tumbling away from her. Jerking her head to the left, she saw Morgan's blankets and sheet ripped away, falling to the floor as he flailed about fighting an invisible enemy. With a moan, she quickly got out of bed. Sleep left her completely as she dodged his flying fists.

"Morgan!" she cried. "Morgan, wake up!"

Through the gunfire and explosion of mortars, Morgan heard a woman's voice. He could smell the blood and the sweat of fear, taste the terror and hear the cries of his men around him. In the midst of it, he felt a cool, strong hand grip his shoulder. He heard a woman's low, husky voice calling him away from that hill in Vietnam. With all his strength, he homed in on her voice, knowing on some deep survival level that she could help him. She could save him from the tragedy unfolding before his tightly shut eyes.

His breath was coming in ragged gasps and sweat rolling down his temples, as he shook like the proverbial leaf in a storm. Blindly, he reached out to grab that cool, steadying hand, to cling to that husky-voiced woman who soothed his raw state. With a groan, he buried his face against her breasts, holding her as if to release her would throw him back into his newly remembered hell. Would the nightmare ever end? Morgan had no idea, at once snared in the bloody memories of the past, and yet clutching her small, strong body, which spoke of the present and hope. Even as he pressed his face against her, feeling the soft give of her breasts beneath the silky material of her gown, the memories kept running before his shut eyes like a reel of movie film.

"It's all right, all right," Laura crooned, stroking Morgan's damp hair. She held him tightly with her other arm, which she'd wrapped around his trembling, rigid body. He clung to her, and her ribs ached beneath the tension of his arms. Explosions of breath tore from him, and she knew he was back in Vietnam. Closing her eyes, resting her cheek against his hair, Laura continued her soothing words and began to rock him gently back and forth, as a mother might a frightened child. It had always worked before when Morgan would get caught up in his virulent nightmares, and she could feel it miraculously working now. Little by little, his grip loosened, his breathing softening to gasps, and she could feel him returning to the present, once more escaping his horrific past.

As she sat on his bed, rocking him, she realized more of the memories from Vietnam must have returned. On one level, it was good news—his mind giving up the information, another piece of his life returning. She compressed her lips, kissing his hair, then his sweaty brow. Would Morgan ever remember her? Remember their love? Laura's heart ached for him—and for herself—as she continued talking softly, knowing her voice would lead him out of his nightmare state and back to the present. Even if he had no memory of her similar help in years past, he was responding positively to it, and she was grateful.

Morgan's heart was beating so hard that for a fleeting moment he feared he'd die of a heart attack. But the bloody hill had at last begun to fade. He'd almost died on that hill, had thought he *was* going to, but he hadn't. He felt a woman's lips pressed against his brow. Who...? *Laura*. His mind gyrated between the freshly churned up Vietnam memories and Laura holding him with her woman's strength and tenderness. He'd tasted death that day. He'd been so sure he was going to die like his men around him.

Something in Morgan screamed out for him to prove he was alive. He saw himself in his blood-soaked green utilities, torn and dirty. He saw himself fighting off five Vietcong who had charged through the last lines of defense to attack him. Morgan felt the butt of an AK-47 as it smashed into the side of his face. He felt numbness, then the strong flow of warm blood down his temple and cheek. He was going to die. He saw it in the eyes of his enemies, who wanted him dead.

In one motion, he released Laura enough to capture her soft mouth. He had to live! He had to feel as if he were more alive than dead! Covering her mouth, he took it—hard and deep. He needed to feel her warmth, her body—feel her responding to him. Her fragrance encircled him, its perfumed scent overriding the odors of blood and death. He felt her moan, the sweet sound vibrating through him, erasing some of the nightmarish past that still clutched at him. Oh, God, let him live! Let him survive this! He slid his hand upward, feeling her small ribs, then groaned as his fingers curved around her small, taut breast.

Mindless, acting only out of the instinct to survive, he tugged impatiently at the strap of the silken nightgown, hearing the fabric give way as he frantically searched for and found her exposed breast. Tearing his mouth from her lips, he settled it on her hardened nipple, suckling there. Life instead of death. Love instead of hatred. He heard her cry out—a cry of pure pleasure—and felt her press him.

The past rushed together with the present—the blood of the past mingling with the blood engorging him until he ached for release within her. He pushed the nightgown away from her body, needing to feel her naked, warm skin against him. Laura was alive. She was here, in his arms. He could feel her fingers digging into his bunched shoulder muscles as he continued to suckle her. Nothing had ever felt so right to him. A fierce desire welled up through him, erasing the nightmare once and for all. In its place, he was aware of her lithe body pressed hotly against him, her fingers opening and closing spasmodically against his shoulders, her small cries of pleasure and the fragrant scent that was only her....

Lifting his mouth from her wet nipple, he took her lips again as he laid her across the bed, needing to seek her womanly core, wanting to feel the heat of her life. He slid his hand down across her smooth belly to ease her thighs apart. Her mouth was soft and giving beneath his, fiercely returning his hungry assault, her breath as ragged and demanding as his. As Morgan slipped his fingers between her damp, taut thighs, he relished the moment as no other. It was one thing to kiss Laura, to suckle her, but to touch her this way was to his dizzied senses, even more intimate, more loving.

As his hand moved between her legs, he felt her stiffen. At first he thought it was her enjoyment of his touch contracting her muscles. Then, he heard Laura gasp his name—the single sound holding an edge of terror. Her fear snapped him out of his state instantly. Lifting his head, he felt a new, unfamiliar vibration tremble through Laura. He might not consciously remember loving her before this moment, but instinctively he knew that what he was feeling now between them wasn't right. It was all wrong. But why?

Morgan looked down to see a terror in Laura's eyes he would never have believed possible. She lay stiffly in his arms, her hands shoving frantically against his chest, as if to push him away. Her lips, still glistening from his kisses, were contorted. It took Morgan precious moments to reorient himself. He felt her terror as if it were his own. What had he done wrong?

"Laura?" His voice sounded harsh as he took his hand away from her thighs and helped her sit up. To his astonishment she crawled away from him, curling into a protective position, her legs against her body, her arms wrapped around herself to hide her naked state from him. She huddled, wildness in her eyes, her back pressed against the pine headboard.

The air was cool. Disgruntled and confused, Morgan pulled the blanket from the floor and wrapped it around her. "Laura? What's wrong? Talk to me. What did I do?"

And as he watched her in the darkness, her face deeply shadowed, her eyes mirroring raw terror, he realized he'd broken his word to her. He'd promised not to touch her—yet he had. Raking his fingers through his hair, Morgan felt ashamed. Caught in the depths of his virulent memories, he'd almost taken her out of selfishness to prove he was more alive than dead inside.

Reaching out slowly, he whispered raggedly, "I'm sorry, Laura... damn, I didn't mean to do this to you.... It was the nightmare, the stuff from Vietnam I was remembering...." His fingers made contact with the edge of the blanket that she gripped so tightly. He wanted to cry over what he'd done to frighten her. Maybe he couldn't recall their love from the past, but dammit, he hadn't meant to scare her like this. He'd never seen Laura look like she did right now.

Wiping his mouth with the back of his hand, he rasped, "I'm sorry, so damn sorry, Laura. I never meant to scare you...."

"It's—not you," Laura gasped out brokenly. "It's me, Morgan. It's me!"

He heard the animal-like sound of her voice and stared at her in the ensuing silence. "What are you talking about? I promised not to touch you until—until I could remember, dammit!" He was angry with himself.

Fighting back a sob, she shook her head. "N-no, you don't understand, Morgan. It's me. It's *my* past that got in the way." A sob tore from her.

Looking at her strangely, he moved closer. "What are you talking about?" He pushed several strands of her hair away from her eyes. "Laura? What is it? I don't understand what you're saying."

Tears burned in Laura's eyes and Morgan's face blurred momentarily before her. She forced out a response. "I don't know what happened, Morgan. I wanted you to kiss me, to touch me...." She shut her eyes, ashamed. "And then... something happened. I was enjoying you, wanting you so badly. But something happened."

"What?" he demanded roughly. "What did I do? Did I hurt you? That's the last thing I'd ever want to do, Laura. You've got to believe me."

Laura gripped the edges of the blanket, feeling so very cold and distraught. Morgan's face mirrored a mix of confusion, concern and anger. She knew the anger was aimed not at her but at himself for some unknown transgression. "The fault," she said unsteadily, "isn't yours. It's mine. You did nothing wrong, Morgan. Absolutely nothing."

"Then..." Morgan shook his head and took her back into his arms. She came without hesitation, huddled against him like a lost, frightened child. "What is it? Talk to me. How can I help you?" He moved his hand up and down her blanketed arm. Laura pressed her face against his chest as if she wanted to hide not only from him, but from herself.

"I—it's the rape, Morgan," she whispered bleakly. "My therapist warned me this might happen, but I didn't believe it. Oh, God, Morgan, I froze when you started to touch me down there. Something inside me just snapped, and I felt myself leaving my body. I felt such terror that I couldn't think. I felt like a cornered animal that was about to die!" She blinked through her tears as she studied his ravaged face in the dim light. "But it was you! I love you! I'm not afraid of you, of your touch." Pressing her hands to her face, she sobbed.

Gently, Morgan held her close, wrapping his arms around her. "Shh," he whispered close to her ear, "it's all right, Laura. It's all right...." It wasn't, but he didn't know what else to say or do. Somehow, Laura's past had been revealed in a way neither had expected. His mind spun with questions, and he felt helpless. And then he felt rage toward Garcia. As he rocked Laura in his arms, whispering words of comfort, renewed fury tunneled through Morgan. At that moment, he wanted to kill the man who had hurt her. He searched his spotty memory for any knowledge about rape, but he knew nothing about its effects. Damn! As if they didn't have enough to handle, Laura's rape had reared its ugly, controlling head, ruining the one, untouched thing they'd been able to share with each other.

Angrily, Morgan sat there, consumed by his hatred of Garcia. He waited until Laura stopped trembling. When he felt her begin to relax against him, he took her over to her bed and made her lie down.

"I'm going to fix us some tea," he told her huskily. "I'll be right back. Just lie there, Laura. Try to relax."

Laura followed Morgan's shadowy presence with her gaze until he disappeared from the chilly room. Grief overwhelmed her. What had her body done to her? Or had it been her mind? How could she reject Morgan, the man she loved so fiercely? How could his touch, which she had so eagerly dreamed of, suddenly make her feel such terror? Morgan hadn't raped her, Garcia had. Repeatedly.

But that wasn't all, Laura knew it. And Morgan still did not know the rest of what had happened. Her grief turned to a deep, gutting sense of loss. In reality, she'd lost Morgan the night he'd been kidnapped. All his memories were returning except for those of her and their marriage. Bitterness coated her mouth as she lay on her side, clenched into a protective fetal position. Tears dampened her eyes as her mind and emotions spun out of control. How could she have pushed Morgan, of all people, away from her?

Laura felt something deep within her shatter—actually felt the snapping sensation in the region of her solar plexus region—leaving in its wake a spiraling sense of giving up, of no longer having the strength to fight back or to survive all that lay ahead for her and Morgan. Of what use was she? Because of the rapes, she would spurn Morgan in the future. Her therapist had warned her but Laura hadn't wanted to believe it—had gone into denial about it. Morgan's kisses had not brought up these feelings of detachment and terror. On the contrary, she had greedily absorbed them and his touch like sunlight into the frozen ground of her broken heart and mortally wounded soul.

A ragged sigh tore from her lips. She could hear Morgan in the kitchen making tea. He didn't remember her, their marriage or their children. Would he ever? Something warned her he wouldn't. But even if he did, so what? The way she was feeling now, unable to allow him to touch her intimately, what good would it do? The feeling of worthlessness grew within Laura until her life stretched before her, grim and gray.

Morgan was a man of great passion. He not only deserved but required a woman who could lie eagerly with him and love him fully. Settling for mere kisses could not be enough. Laura realized sadly she couldn't be the woman he needed.

She was, in the true sense of the word, damaged merchandise. And Morgan didn't even know the worst of it yet. A sob tore from her throat and she pressed her face into the pillow, wanting to die, wanting to escape the overwhelming pain that had finally broken her. She had no more strength left, no more will to fight back and survive. Garcia had murdered her, she realized, grief stricken by the dawning awareness. He'd taken her physically and killed her emotionally. His evil revenge was still playing itself out.

Sobbing harder, the sounds absorbed by the pillow, Laura realized for the first time the extent of the revenge Garcia had leveled against Morgan. The drug lord had known that by raping her, he was taking her from Morgan. The very thing Morgan loved most in the world—his wife—was gone forever. As Laura tried to stop crying before Morgan came back with the tea, she realized it was probably a lucky thing that he no longer recalled their life together, for it could only cause him greater pain now.

Oh, how could he live with such hurt? She couldn't. She knew that what they'd shared could never again be the same—ever. Why put him through it? Hadn't he suffered enough? Wouldn't it be better if she simply disappeared? A shadow of the past that remained there? That way, Laura thought, he could get on with his life. He could find a woman he could love—who would love him fully in return.

Yes, that was the answer. She had to leave. Who would want her the way she was—frigid, fearing a man's intimate touch? Morgan didn't remember her anyway. And now the terrible, wrenching secret she still carried would stay safe with her. Morgan need never know. To cut out the pain that only grew daily between them, Laura became increasingly convinced that she must leave as soon as possible. Somehow, she would disappear. No one, not even her children, must know where she'd gone, though just the thought of never seeing Jason and Katherine again made her sob even harder.

Still, Laura convinced herself, Susannah Killian would care for them, would be a wonderful surrogate mother until Morgan could find another woman to love him without the baggage of the past overwhelming their present. Yes, her children were young; they would adjust. But could she? Laura wasn't certain. But she was sure she had to leave. It would be best this way—for all involved.

Chapter Eleven

Sunlight lanced brightly into the bedroom, eventually wakening Morgan. He raised his head, blinking, and pushed his covers off. What time was it? Disgruntled, he sat up, feeling exhausted. Leaning over, his hands covering his face, he allowed the memories of the night before to return. Shame intertwined with guilt as he thought about his selfish, almost instinctive actions with Laura. Where the hell was his head? Why hadn't he placed her rape squarely in front of him instead of behind him, practically denying it had happened?

Sourly, Morgan lifted his head and rubbed his hands along his thighs as he stared at the sunshine spilling through the east window. Laura's bed was empty. She usually got up and moved about sooner than he did of late. He heard the short, sharp exchanges of chickadees outside, and the soothing sounds of the nearby creek. A momentary peace settled over him. He liked being so near water. Maybe he should move the family to the ocean. He wondered what Laura would say to that idea.

Hell, he didn't even remember if Laura liked the ocean. Today he was going to drop by and talk to Dr. Parsons—see if he could cultivate an understanding of what rape did to a woman and how to handle it. He wasn't about to put Laura through that kind of anguish again—at least, not knowingly.

As he sat thinking about her, Morgan began to realize that what he felt toward Laura was far more than caring. Something alive and healthy remained between them despite the terrible circumstances that now engulfed them. Morgan felt that vibration of certainty in his heart, which seemed to expand with absolute joy. Though his mind might refuse to release the memory of loving her, he knew now, sitting on the edge of his bed, that he loved her anyway.

The feeling exploded through him, flooding him with a wonderful sensation. Yes, he loved her. When had it happened? Morgan couldn't honestly pinpoint a day or an hour when his feelings had shifted from care to love. Excitement thrummed through him. It didn't matter now whether he recalled their past love, because it had somehow been transferred from his past into his present. It had just happened.

Gratefully, he closed his eyes, resting his hands on his thighs as he savored his discovery. Up until this moment, he'd been careful not to say the word *love* to Laura. He hadn't wanted to hurt her or raise false hopes. Now Morgan realized he could honestly get up, leave this room and go tell Laura, to her face, that he loved her.

The corners of his mouth tipped upward as he savored that forthcoming duty. What would she do? Would her deep blue eyes sparkle with those flecks of gold? She had such a soft mouth. He would watch the joy shimmer through her and absorb the beauty of her tremulous smile. With this latest revelation, they were freed from the past. Laura had told him she loved him, but he hadn't reciprocated. Now he could!

Eagerly, Morgan got to his feet. He didn't hear Laura stirring in the cabin, but that wasn't unusual. She would often wake up before him, take her bath, dress and go for a walk, then come back and make breakfast for them. By that time, he'd be up, showered, shaved and ready to start his day—with her. Hope tunneled through him as he retrieved some clean clothes from the drawer and padded through the warm living room to the bathroom. Stopping, he poked his head into the kitchen. Laura wasn't there, but he smelled the coffee she'd made earlier, and it made his mouth water. First, he'd shower and dress.

Glancing at his watch after he'd showered and shaved, Morgan saw it was nearly nine o'clock. Today he'd chosen a dark blue chamois shirt, fresh jeans and his usual hiking boots. Glancing in the mirror, still ringed with humidity from his shower, he quickly combed his short, black hair into place. A smile tugged at his mouth as he studied himself. What an ugly-looking bastard he was, with that scar running the length of one side of his face. Yet Laura loved him. Unequivocally. Forever. The feeling in his heart, that newly pulsing warmth, hadn't stopped since he'd realized his love for her. If anything, it was even stronger now, more anticipatory, because Morgan wanted so badly to share it with her.

After last night's fiasco, when he'd wounded her by his ignorant, selfish actions, Morgan wanted to make her happy, to take away the terror he'd seen in her eyes and replace it with wonder. Humming to himself, he stepped out of the bathroom, his boots echoing down the short hall. He halted in the living room doorway. The radio wasn't on. They picked up a great FM station out of Prescott, which Laura usually turned on when she returned from her walk. The living room remained quiet.

Morgan scowled, feeling uneasy without knowing why. Maybe Laura was back in the bedroom, lying down, still shattered by last night's experience. Worry began to edge into the joy thrumming through him as he walked back to their bedroom. His hands resting against the doorframe, Morgan looked around the room. It was empty. Laura had to be in the kitchen, though he didn't pick up the normal sounds of her making breakfast. Shoving away his growing anxiety, he walked into the kitchen.

A glance told him it, too, was empty. His gaze swept the small area, catching something out of place on the table. A piece of paper was propped up between the salt and pepper shakers. His anxiety heightened savagely as he walked over to the table. Reaching for the paper, he saw Laura's flowery handwriting and gave the note his full attention.

My Darling Morgan,
I don't know how to begin or end this letter. It's

so painful to write. Anymore, I don't seem to know what I'm doing. I used to think I knew right from wrong, day from night, black from white, but I don't. Darling, please forgive me for what I've done. Last night I felt something so intrinsic within me break that I feel disconnected. Perhaps I've gone insane. I truly don't know.

When you awoke out of your Vietnam nightmare, I knew that more of your past had come back. No one could be happier than I was when you took me in your arms and started to make love to me. I couldn't believe it was happening, because in the past, we often made love after you came out of those nightmares. For you, it was a way to prove you were alive, and I understood that and *wanted* you to love me.

But suddenly, last night, I didn't want you loving me. I couldn't stand the thought of being touched—even by you. Images of being raped flashed before me, and I couldn't make them go away. I couldn't concentrate enough on the fact that it was you loving me. Oh, Morgan, I'm so sorry. I feel so horrible, so out of control. I left my body at some point—was completely disconnected from you—and that's never happened before. I felt violated. I knew you weren't my rapist, yet my body and emotions responded as if you were.

I can't go on this way, Morgan. God knows, you don't deserve it. Right now, I can't stand the agony. I thought I knew what hurt was, but I didn't. I thought I was in pain during my captivity with Garcia, or after I was rescued and we tried to find Jason. Then I thought getting our son back would ease the pain, but it didn't. It just multiplied because I didn't know if you were alive. But the children kept me going. They needed a parent, and I clung to that fact.

When Perseus found you, I went through the pain of waiting. I lived moment to moment, more uncertain than ever before. How badly I wanted what we had to come back! And what if you were dead? When Culver and Pilar rescued you, and we received the call that you were alive, I felt a joy that made me faint for a moment. And I thought that finally the pain would leave. But when Ann told me that you had suffered damage to your memory, the pain was worse than ever.

These past few weeks with you at the cabin have been heaven and hell for me, Morgan. I've tried so hard to do the right thing, say the right thing, but little by little, whatever strength I had has slowly oozed out of me. Last night broke me. I realized then that nothing I did or didn't do was going to help you. Morgan, I'm not the Laura you knew and can't remember. I'm broken inside. I don't know who I am any longer. I can't look to you for help because you're struggling so hard to heal yourself. You don't need me around, causing you pain. Right now, I feel crazed. The hurt is so horrible that I feel insane with it.

I've decided to leave. It is the hardest thing I've ever done, but I believe I'm doing it for the right reasons—or at least I think I am. I'm not really sure about much these days. It's a relief to me that you don't remember our past, because I've

changed so much since my kidnapping and rapes.
You need a warm, loving, giving woman to help
you through your trauma, and I no longer have
the strength to be that for you. If I stayed, Morgan, I'd become an albatross around your neck—
just another responsibility and liability to carry
while you're trying to heal. I love you too much
to do that to you.

Worse, I never told you the full truth about the
rapes. I was afraid to tell you that the doctor examined me and told me I could never have another child; the damage done to me was too great.
For me, that was the ultimate sentence, Morgan.
I love children so much, and we had wanted at
least four. Before the kidnapping, we were planning our third baby. We even had names picked
out. I'd be useless to you in that way—frigid and
sterile. What man in his right mind wants a
woman like me around?

It's early in the morning, and I'm leaving.
Please ask Susannah to continue to take care of
Jason and Katherine. I cried so much at the
thought of never seeing them again. But I know
my decision is for the best. I don't want our children ever to know the hell inside me. I'm afraid
I'd lose control, and I don't want to hurt them or
you. None of you deserve this. Please don't try to
find me, Morgan. Let me go. I hope that my
leaving will ultimately help everyone.

I don't know what I'm going to do or where I'll
go. Please forgive me, Morgan. I don't know
what else to do. I love you. I love Jason and
Katherine. I pray that someday your memory will

return and you'll love them as much as you did
before. You were a wonderful father to them, and
I know you can be again.

Goodbye...

                                            Love, Laura

"Son of a bitch!" Violently, Morgan spun on his
heel. The paper fluttered to the table as he reached for
the phone on the wall, his heart pounding with unri-
valed pain. The joy he'd felt was destroyed, in its place
raw, primal agony. No! Laura didn't know what she
was doing! He grabbed the phone, his hand shaking
as he dialed the ranch.

"Rachel? This is Morgan. Let me talk to Ann. It's
an emergency."

The next few minutes were an unfolding nightmare
as he stood tensely in the kitchen, telling Ann about
the letter Laura had left.

"What the hell's going on?" he demanded tightly.

"She's had a temporary break from reality," Ann
said worriedly. "I was afraid something like this might
happen. Laura's therapist said she wasn't getting anywhere with her, that Laura had gone into deep denial
over the rapes. It's typical of her to push her own
problems and feelings aside in favor of her family's
needs. She hasn't been taking care of herself first,
Morgan, and this is the result. It's a highly codepen-
dent response, and Laura isn't the only woman who
has that problem, believe me."

His hand tightened on the phone receiver until his
knuckles whitened. "Is she going to kill herself?"

"It doesn't sound like it—at least, not yet. Right
now she's trying to run away from the pain. Later,

when she discovers she can't outrun it, is when the suicidal impulse could set in."

"Dammit!" he rasped. "Why didn't I realize all this? Why didn't I—"

"Morgan, you're both hurting. It's especially hard when both parties are at a survival level and trying to put the pieces of their lives back together. It's impossible for either of you be there fully for your partner. My hunch is that Laura tried to do that, to be everything for you, and in doing so, she used up the extra hope, love and energy she needed for her own recovery. She was on the edge, anyway. That's why I kept coming by to check on you two—I was more concerned about her than you."

"I was stable because she was feeding me with her attention, love and care," he growled angrily. Why the hell hadn't he realized that? In effect, Laura had been transfusing him with her lifeblood: he grew stronger, she was slowly dying right before his eyes—and he hadn't seen it. He knotted his fist, agony exploding through his chest. He heard Ann's voice—and tried to focus on what she was saying.

"Got to find her. Do you have any idea where she might have gone? Did she have a favorite place here?"

"I—I don't know," he answered, looking around the kitchen. "Her coat is gone. She has a couple hundred bucks. That's enough to get to a bus and head for God knows where."

"Sedona's the closest town," Ann said. "Still, she has to walk out of this place, Morgan. Let me get Mike on the radio. We need to start a search. I'll call the sheriff. They can begin looking for hitchhikers along Route 89, which heads into Sedona and Flagstaff."

Suddenly, an idea struck him. "Wait!" he exclaimed. "I think I know where she might have gone. It would be one way of getting off the ranch and to the highway." Quickly telling Ann his idea, he hung up the phone and ran through the cabin. He jerked the door open and began racing along the creek.

The morning was cool and his breath came in white explosions as he paralleled the stream, dodging the rocks and boulders that seemed determined to slow his progress. Breathing harshly, his heart pounding, he tried to calm down and think clearly. Two days ago, it had rained. The soil here was clay, still damp and impressionable. He stopped momentarily and looked around at the muddy ground, trying to control his agony and fear for Laura. She didn't wear hiking boots, which would have left deep impressions in the soil. No, even though she had boots, she favored an old pair of plain leather oxfords that she'd laughingly told him were more comfortable—"like old friends."

Morgan stopped and rubbed his brow. The shoes were specially made, with an emblem carved into the sole though they had no tread to speak of. Breathing hard, he shut his eyes and brought that symbol forward. All he could remember was that it was circular. Opening his eyes, he crouched down. Everywhere Morgan looked, he saw the hoofprints of cattle that roamed along the creek in search of grass and water. He could find no evidence of Laura's shoe print, but perhaps she had taken a diagonal route instead of the path they'd trod previously.

The sun beating down was making Morgan sweat as he checked his watch. It was eleven o'clock. He wiped his mouth with the back of his hand and looked around the scenic area. The red and white cliffs with their black lava caps rose thousands of feet around him, the dark trees standing out against them in brilliant splash of greens. The sky, a deep blue, reminded him of Laura's wide, innocent eyes.

Morgan began to run again, feeling his own strength diminishing with each stride. He knew with a gut feeling where Laura had gone: to that pool. Vividly, he remembered showing her on a map, after they'd returned from their picnic, that the deer path that wound up the cliff on the far side of the pool eventually led to Route 89A. She must have taken it.

Praying he was right, Morgan pushed himself as never before. He had everything to lose; his weakening body had to respond! He loved Laura. He wanted her back. She had to know that! As he ran, his arms pumping, Morgan stumbled on some loose rocks and felt tears streaming down his cheeks. My God, he couldn't lose Laura now. Not after all they'd endured together! A scream began to uncurl deep in his gut, a scream of fury at the turn of events that had been thrown at them. Nothing mattered anymore to Morgan. Nothing but Laura, and getting her back, safe and sound, in his arms.

His heart felt as if it were going to burst in his chest as he ran, drunkenly now, toward the pool. Breathing raggedly in gasps, he stumbled to a halt, anxiously looking around. He'd run three miles, and he was trembling with exhaustion. His lower legs cramped, the pain floating up to his awareness, but not stopping him. As he stood rigidly on the bank, anxiously looking around the pool, he choked.

His eyes narrowed and his heart slammed hard into his ribs. There, across the pool, halfway up the steepest part of the deer trail, lay Laura, apparently unconscious. In those split seconds, a tremendous amount of the past flashed back to Morgan, overwhelming him. His cry echoed through the area. Plunging into the cold, icy water, he lunged forward, his hands stretched toward her. Laura lay unmoving, like a broken rag doll, half on the trail, the rest of her body hidden in the thick, green manzanita bushes that lined it.

Morgan never felt the water's icy temperature. He lunged roughly through the sometimes waist-deep pool to reach the other side, his cry of pure terror echoing and re-echoing around him. As he thrashed the pool, memories of Laura avalanched through him. Pictures and fragments of the past—how they'd met, fallen in love—overwhelmed his panicked senses. As he reached the other side, he stumbled, falling to his hands and knees. He crawled out of the water as the memories of their children sheared back upon him.

As he staggered to his feet, the water rushing down his pant legs and squishing in his hiking boots, Morgan vividly recalled the agonizing hours when Laura had nearly died in labor with Jason. She'd hemorrhaged unexpectedly after the birth. Morgan had been there, had gone into shock as all hell broke loose in the delivery room. He'd stood with a newly blanketed Jason in his hands, watching Laura's face go waxen within moments, due to the heavy loss of blood.

Oh, God, that's how she looked to him now! She was a quarter of a mile up the narrow, steep trail, unmoving. Even as he scrambled, clawing at anything he could get his hands on to reach her faster, Morgan thought she was dead.

Another vignette sheared through him, leaving him sobbing. Morgan remembered how anxious and worried he'd been while Laura carried Katherine. How many nightmares he'd had about her dying during the delivery of their second child. Worse, Laura had gone into premature labor with her. Morgan remembered the pain of thinking he might lose them as he'd paced the hospital's visitor area. Laura had refused a cesarean, though her doctor wanted to perform the operation to keep Laura safe from the possibility of hemorrhaging again. This time they might not be so lucky. This time she could die.

Morgan gasped. Only a few yards to go! Memories overlapped the present, and he remembered Dr. Jane Holly smiling triumphantly as she came out of the delivery room. Little Katherine Alyssa was fine, despite being a month early. Even better, this second birthing process had gone without a hitch, and Laura was not only fine, but asking for him.

Oh! Morgan recalled how he'd run to that delivery room and seen his baby daughter resting on Laura's belly. He remembered Laura's eyes filled with tears of joy as he leaned down to slide his arm beneath her and hold her. They'd cried together—he out of relief that she was alive, and she because Katherine was so perfect and beautiful.

Morgan shook his head, forcing away the wave of memories. He could see now that several rocks had evidently loosened as Laura had tried to scramble up the trail. She had slipped in her smooth-bottomed shoes. As he climbed to where she lay, his gaze riveted on her. Was she dead? She couldn't be! What a horrible way to end such a beautiful, wonderful life. He loved her so much that it hurt him to breathe in that moment.

As he fell to his knees beside Laura and reached out with a shaking hand, Morgan knew she was dead. Her skin was waxen, with a grayish cast. Her lips were parted, her arms hanging lifelessly, her legs tangled in the red branches of the thick manzanita that had stopped her plunge to the bottom of the cliff.

As Morgan felt for a pulse, he sobbed in grief. He would do anything—*anything*—to have Laura alive!

Chapter Twelve

"I love you, Laura. Do you hear me? I love you...."

Groggily, Laura opened her eyes. Morgan's tense face hovered close to hers, and she felt the strength and warmth of his body surrounding her, supporting her. What had happened? Almost as soon as she asked the question, the information filtered through her shorted-out senses. Her head aching abominably, she struggled to sit up. Morgan eased her upward, using his body to support her back, his arm around her shoulders.

"Are you all right?" he demanded, breathing raggedly. Pushing several strands of muddied hair off her face, he searched her pale features. "Laura?"

"Y-yes, I'm okay...." On one level, she was. On many others, she wasn't. Weakly, she raised her hand

and rubbed the back of her head. "I—I must have fallen—"

"You fell, all right," Morgan rasped, glancing down the dangerous trail. He saw where she'd slipped on the slick red clay. Devoting all his attention to her, he said unsteadily, "My God, you could have been killed, Laura."

She hung her head as hot tears pressed at her closed eyelids. The terror in Morgan's voice ripped through her. No longer did she have the strength to stop anything from wounding her further.

"Any broken bones?" he asked hoarsely, running his hands gently over her extremities. "Anything pulled?"

Laura sat in the harbor of his embrace, dazed and unable to think as quickly as he did. But the mere touch of Morgan's hands helped soothe her chaotic state. Bitterly, she realized she couldn't even run away successfully. She vaguely remembered a branch sticking out on the steep deer trail. She'd seen it, but had disregarded it and stepped on it. The stick had rolled and so had she. The last thing she remembered was having her feet fly out from beneath her and landing hard on her back.

Opening her eyes, Laura laughed a little hysterically. "The only thing broken in me is my mind...."

Worriedly, Morgan assessed her eyes, which appeared dark and lifeless. "Hold on," he growled, then picked her up as if she weighed nothing. Steadying himself on the narrow path, he got his bearings, holding her tightly against him. He heard her gasp, her arms going around his neck, but within moments, she relaxed against him, trusting him totally. Well, this time, Morgan decided, he wasn't going to let her down. Gingerly, he picked his way back down the path to the edge of the pool.

"Hang on, you're going for a ride," he warned huskily. She clung to him like a frightened child now, her face buried against his neck. Carefully, he moved through the water, bringing her safely to the other side. It would take another forty minutes to reach the cabin, and he knew his arms would ache like hell itself from carrying Laura that distance, but he sensed she had given up and wouldn't have the strength to walk on her own.

He struck out on the trail that led back to the cabin. "Listen to me," he said roughly near her ear, "listen to what I have to say, Laura." His hand tightened around her thin form. "I remember. I remember us." His voice was unsteady with feelings. "After I read your letter, I thought you might have gone back to the pool where we'd picnicked. As I ran up to the pool and saw you, everything started coming back about us, Laura. Do you hear me? I remember how we met, what happened. Dammit, I remember my love for you!"

Blinking through her tears, Laura lifted her face and looked up at Morgan. Each step he took jarred her, increasing the pain in her head. But miraculously, with his shocking words, the pain left momentarily as she homed in on his raggedly given admission. "Y-you remember?" she asked, afraid to believe what she'd heard. He cut a glance at her, his stride shortening.

"Yes, I remember. *Everything,* Laura." The corners of his mouth turned downward and his voice roughened. "All I want is for you to stay with me.

Don't try to run off again. Do you hear me? All these months you've had to be strong for everyone else. Well, that's changed now. I'm going to be strong for *you*. Do you understand what I'm saying? You need some care and support. Dammit, I didn't mean to take from you the way I did. I didn't realize... honest to God, I didn't. But it won't happen again, and that's a promise, Laura. Looking back over the past seven years, I can see that I've always taken from you and depended on you—without giving you back half of what I got." His mouth compressed. "Well, all that's changing. Right now."

Laura sighed and rested her brow wearily against his jaw. Was she dreaming? Hallucinating? She knew she'd crossed the line somewhere in that unmarked territory between what was real and what wasn't. What could she trust? Tears dribbled down her cheeks, she tasted the salt of them as they followed the outline of her lips.

"Y-you read the letter I left?" she asked, her voice scratchy. Laura felt completely unable to protect herself from whatever Morgan might think about that letter. By rights, he should be angry.

"I read it," he said, his eyes narrowing as he paid strict attention to where he was placing his feet along the trail. Sunlight cascaded down among the branches of the tall pines, and shadows and light danced across Laura as Morgan carried her rapidly toward their cabin. "I read it," he repeated harshly, "and you know what? I don't care if you can't have any more children. We already have two beautiful children. We should count our blessings for what we have, Laura."

He risked a glance down at her and for the first time saw a glimmer of hope in her dark blue eyes.

Morgan could tell Laura was waiting for his anger, but he felt none toward her. "I could kill Garcia with my bare hands," he rasped. "If I ever get the chance, he's a dead man. I'm so damned sorry about what happened to you, Laura." His voice broke. "So damned sorry."

Laura tightened her hold around his neck and powerful shoulders. "I was so afraid, Morgan…so afraid to tell you…."

"I wish you had told me," he said thickly. "But I know why you didn't, too, and it doesn't matter anymore, Laura." He cast another quick glance down at her. "What matters is you. That's all. Everything else in our lives can go to hell." His arms tightened briefly around her, and he watched more of the tension dissolve from her eyes. How he loved her! The powerful, unfolding feelings in his chest were still hitting him in tidal wave proportions as nuances of old memories kept returning, one on top of another. But sorting through all of them was of minor importance in comparison to Laura and her mental and emotional condition. All he wanted in the world in that moment was to get her back to the cabin, call Dr. Parsons and get Laura some help.

"Well?" Morgan demanded in a low tone after Dr. Parsons quietly shut the door to the bedroom, where Laura was resting.

Ann smiled gently and guided Morgan to the living room couch, where she sat down with him. Mike Houston had brought her to the cabin, and he stood worriedly in the kitchen doorway, a cup of coffee in hand.

"I gave her a tranquilizer, Morgan. She's already asleep. She's exhausted from everything that's happened."

"What did happen?"

Ann picked up the note. "Basically, in layperson's terms, she gave up. I'm sorry, I didn't know she hadn't told you about her physical complications from the rapes. I thought you knew."

He shook his head and folded his hands between his thighs. "She said she was afraid to tell me."

"I can understand why," Ann murmured as she set the note aside. "But the worst is out in the open now. No more skeletons remain in either of your closets, so to speak. You're finally sharing a level playing field. You remember your past with Laura, your marriage and your children, so that's a very healthy start toward healing all that's happened to both of you."

Worriedly, Morgan rasped, "What about Laura, though? I know she hates to take any kind of drugs. I hate to see her on antidepressants or tranquilizers— even if she'll take them."

Reaching out, Ann patted his shoulder. "It's only temporary, Morgan. Right now, you're Laura's antidepressant."

"What do you mean?"

"When she wakes up, which probably won't be for a good eight hours, let her talk. You just sit and listen. When she needs reassurance, give it to her. But keep in mind that she felt abandoned, out there all alone with this big, bad world looming over her, slowly crushing the life out of her. Try to be more aware of when you're placing demands on her, and try not to. She's given too much to too many people for too long. It's time she came first, not second or last.''

''That was my gut feeling about all this,'' he admitted harshly, angry all over again at his role in putting Laura in such a position in the first place. ''Damn,'' he growled, running his fingers distractedly through his hair, ''I'm one selfish son of a bitch.''

Laughing gently, Ann got up. ''A healthy response, Morgan. And yes, you've been pretty demanding on Laura over the years. She always came second to Perseus, too.''

His eyes narrowed on the physician. ''You're right,'' he said finally.

Ann's smile increased as she put her medical items back into her black leather bag. ''I've never accused you of being slow, Morgan. I think you've got the big picture now. You know what needs to be done to help Laura through this, so she can put her life back together. Mike's going to take me back to the ranch, but I'll leave some sleeping pills and a few tranquilizers, in case Laura needs them. She probably won't touch them, but they're here, just in case.''

Mike came over and picked up Ann's bag for her.

''I prescribe R and R for both of you in the next week,'' Ann added. ''If you or Laura want me to come back out, call. Otherwise, I'm keeping a low profile.''

Morgan nodded. ''Thanks, Ann—for everything.'' And he meant that—she'd been a steady light in their darkness. ''You're one hell of a flight surgeon. Did I ever tell you that?'' He saw Ann's face flush and pleasure come to her eyes as Mike opened the door for her.

"No, but it's nice to hear it—finally. We'll see you later...."

Morgan sat in the silence of the cabin after Ann and Mike had left. Harshly, he rubbed his face. He'd come so close to losing the one thing he loved most in the world. Getting up, stiff from the extreme exercise of the morning, he went into the kitchen to pour himself some coffee. Memories and emotions were continuing to roll over him, more than ever now that his focus wasn't needed elsewhere.

How long he sat at the kitchen table, the cup of coffee growing cold between his hands, Morgan didn't know. Most of the emotions he experienced during those hours were good ones. Rich ones filled with happiness, hope and laughter. They'd shared some bad times, too—especially when Laura had nearly died in childbirth. Morgan felt a bitter taste in his mouth. Damn, he'd nearly lost her again—in a different way.

A lot had to change, he realized. And he had to be the one to do it—for Laura, for himself and for their family. First, though, he had to reestablish that broken connection with Laura. She had to believe he remembered and fully felt his love for her. Would she? Morgan was no longer sure of anything. He could only wait and see.

When Laura awoke, it was dark outside. The cabin was warm, and she noticed the door to the bedroom was open, the heat from the earth stove filtering into the room. Oddly, she felt not only warm, but safe and even happy. Happy? As she rubbed her face and drowsily sat up to push the covers away, she remembered what had happened, and her small flicker of happiness died. Fear replaced it—and anxiety. Where was Morgan? Laura didn't hear anything except the soft music of the Prescott FM station she loved. The music helped soothe her anxiety to a degree as she forced herself to get up.

Pulling on her chenille robe, she slowly made her way into the living room. Morgan was sitting on the couch near the stove, one of the family photo albums spread open across his lap. The light from the nearby floor lamp deepened and emphasized the ruggedness of his features. How much she loved him! Her heart pounded with the knowledge as she stood absorbing his strong, powerful presence back into her life.

He must have sensed she was up because suddenly his chin lifted and his gray eyes narrowed on her. Laura managed a broken smile. Almost instantly, he was on his feet, striding toward her, an anxious look replacing the intent concentration of moments before. Without speaking, he gripped her by her upper arms and assessed her.

"How are you feeling?" he asked huskily after a few moments' study.

"A little out of sorts," Laura whispered, allowing her hands to rest on his arms. "Is it true, Morgan? Or did I make it up or dream it?"

"What?" Morgan saw the fragility in her eyes and heard it in her low, husky voice.

"That you remember . . . us? The children?"

He smiled a little. "Yeah, everything came back this morning when I was looking for you, Little Swan."

Laura swayed. Closing her eyes, she felt his grip tighten on her arms. "Little Swan" was Morgan's special endearment for her. Tears threatened to choke her. "Oh," she whispered unsteadily, smiling up at him, "you do remember. You really do...."

Whispering her name, Morgan brought Laura into his arms and held her gently against him, kissing her mussed hair. "I really do," he assured her gruffly. "You're my Little Swan with the long, beautiful neck and the grace of a ballerina." He buried his face in her hair. "God," he rasped, "I love you so much, Laura. So much it hurts." His embrace tightened, and he felt her tremble violently, once, at his admission. He managed a choked laugh. "In fact, I'm afraid you're going to get sick and tired of me telling you how much I love you."

"N-no," Laura quavered, sliding her arms around his waist, "I'll never get enough of you telling me that, Morgan. Not ever..."

Gently, he placed his hand against the clean line of her jaw and guided her lips to his. It was so natural, so easy between them, to cover her lips and feel the softness that had always been her—to feel her tentative response to his mouth taking hers. But Morgan was aware of her fragile state more than ever. Even the way she returned his kiss was hesitant. Because of the rape? Because she thought he was Garcia and was unable to separate them? Right now, it didn't matter to Morgan. All Laura had to understand was that he was back. He was home, finally—for her and their children.

Easing his mouth from her lips, he smiled deeply into her lustrous eyes. "I love you," he said thickly.

"And no matter what's happened, Laura, I'll always love you." He threaded his fingers through her tangled blond hair. "That's never going to change, Little Swan, so no matter what you're feeling, or what hell we still have to walk through together, never let go of that fact. All right?"

Laura nodded, her hands resting against his massive chest. "All right."

"Do you believe me?"

She smiled a little. "I believe you, Morgan."

"Good," he said, satisfied. "Then let's get you a bath. From here on out, you're number one in this marriage, not number two. That's changing as of this moment."

Laura had no idea what Morgan was talking about, but she found out soon enough. Not only did he draw her a tub of hot water with her favorite orange crystals in it, he washed her hair for her. When they had first been married, Morgan had done that for her from time to time, and Laura had loved it. She had luxuriated in his care of her—and now she got to do so again. Completely surprised by the change in him, she reeled a little in shock from it all. But Morgan pressed on, making her a late dinner of T-bone steak, mashed potatoes and salad. Though she didn't feel very hungry, he sat with her, cajoling each bite of food into her mouth and not allowing her to leave the table until at least half of it had been consumed.

Later, as she lay on the huge sheepskin rug, her back to the warmth of the stove and only the flickering of the flames lighting the cabin, Laura felt hope trickling back into her heart. Morgan had provided a pillow for her head, and it felt good just to lie on the rug and be warm and safe—and loved. He was washing the dishes, and the pleasant sounds emanating from the kitchen lulled her into a light sleep.

She felt more than heard him coming into the living room. Sleepily, she opened her eyes and saw him sit down, his long legs spread out parallel to her, a piece of chocolate cake with two scoops of vanilla ice cream in hand. A smile played across her lips as she eased into a sitting position.

"There's no secret to you," she teased huskily, pushing her hair away from her face and crossing her legs.

"Any secrets I ever carried, you know about," Morgan said seriously. He dipped the spoon into the ice cream. "Here, have some."

Laura was about to protest, but seeing the glint in his dark eyes she thought better of it. Instead she opened her mouth and allowed Morgan to slide the spoon between her lips. The ice cream was sweet and soothing.

"Mmm, that's good," she admitted gratefully.

He smiled a little. "You need to gain back that twenty pounds you've lost, Laura. You look too much like a prisoner of war."

Moving slowly, Laura propped herself next to him, her back against the couch, her shoulder and hip touching his. The silence was soft and without incrimination as Morgan shared his cake and ice cream with her—a sensual, delicious and unexpected experience for Laura. Sighing softly afterward, she was contented and let Morgan place his arm around her and draw her against him.

"This is heaven," she whispered, sliding her arm around him in return.

"It doesn't get better than this," he agreed thickly, placing a kiss on her hair.

With a shake of her head, Laura said hesitantly, "I feel as if we're starting all over again, Morgan."

Taking her hand and placing it against his thigh, he gently caressed her skin. "In a way we are, Little Swan."

"I'm so scared...."

"So am I." Morgan studied her in the warming silence. "So we'll be scared together, okay?" He was relieved to see the hope burning in her eyes once more. One thing about Laura: she might be strong, and God knew she was a warrior of the first order when it came to fighting for her family, but when she crashed, it was complete. He'd seen her surrender once before, when she'd nearly died after Jason was born. With his help and care, a miracle had taken place within her: she'd rallied, flourishing remarkably well in a short time.

He didn't really expect her to rally so quickly this time, but already he was seeing signs of her responding to him—just as before. Grateful beyond words, Morgan cupped her face and held her tear-filled gaze. "We have a lot to work through, sweetheart. I know the rapes stand between us, but with therapy for both of us, and working together, we'll one day make all of that a part of our past, too. I've talked to Ann about what rape does to a woman, and she made me see clearly how it affects not only you, but me."

"And our marriage," Laura murmured softly, her fingers digging into the fabric of his shirt.

"Yes. Rape affects everyone." He caressed her flushed cheek. "And neither of us is going to go into denial about it. Ann said it often takes at least a year to get over the worst effects, and time slowly takes care of the rest. I know," he told her somberly, "that I can't make love with you right now. It's impossible for you to emotionally separate what happened from our being together. But one day, Ann said, we will be able to enjoy making love together again, Laura, and it's a day I know will come. I don't care how long it takes. You've got to believe me on that, Little Swan. I didn't marry you just to have you in my bed."

"No?" Her smile was broken and fragile.

"No. Although—" Morgan whispered, kissing her lips tenderly, "it's a natural way to express our love for each other. But there are plenty of other ways I can show my love for you, and vice versa. I see this as an opportunity to explore those other ways."

"I—I don't like separate beds, Morgan."

His smile was very male and very gentle. "No?"

Laura shook her ahead adamantly. "I hated sleeping apart from you. I need you to hold me at night. If you could do that—"

"You just tell me whatever you need, and I'll provide it, Laura," he vowed fiercely. "Ann says we've got to talk, to communicate like never before. I know I haven't been very good at it the past seven years, but I'm going to get good at it now." He brushed the tears from her cheeks. "You know what this whole thing has taught me, Little Swan?"

"No...what?"

"Well, for one thing, that you and our children are more important to me than my work." He shook his head apologetically. "I didn't realize until now how much. I put work before you and our family. But all that's coming to a roaring halt, Laura."

Startled, she studied him in the warm darkness. "What are you talking about?" she whispered unsteadily.

Pressing her against him, Morgan rested his jaw lightly against her hair. "While you were sleeping, I made a lot of decisions, Little Swan. Among them is that I'm going to sell Perseus to the government. They've wanted to buy in as a partner before, but now I'm going to sell them the whole thing. I know I can wrangle a financially sound deal for us, and I'll write operation manuals for them, but beyond that I'm taking a back seat for now.

"We need time to heal. Our children need us, and we need them. When you're ready, we're going to Jake Randolph's place. He's already agreed to act as liaison between the CIA, which will be purchasing Perseus, and myself. You and I will go up to Oregon, to the Cascade Mountains, and the kids will join us there. We're going to spend the next three months living there—Jake figures it will take at least that long to perform the transition work between the company and the CIA, and he'll stay in D.C. doing it. His Oregon home is big and has plenty of bedrooms. We'll have the privacy we need, too."

Laura lay against Morgan, almost unable to believe what she was hearing. The gruff emotional quality of Morgan's voice felt like a thick, protective blanket over her rawness. "I never thought you'd give up Perseus," she said finally, after a hushed silence.

"In a way I won't. The government will use my knowledge, tactics and strategies in the manuals I'll continue to write and refine. But most importantly, this change will remove us as a target, and that's what I want."

Laura could hear Morgan's commitment to her and their family in his fervent voice. She tightened her arms around him briefly. "I miss the children so much," she whispered.

"So do I," he rasped. "I want to hold that little tiger of a son of mine in my arms again, and I want to smell Katherine's fresh, clean scent as I carry her."

Hope exploded into Laura's heart. The sensation of warmth that followed it was completely unexpected, yet she savored the feeling, greedily absorbing it. "I like your decisions," she said faintly. "I feel like I'm in a waking dream. You don't know how many times I wished you would put your work aside for our family."

Grimly, Morgan stared out into the darkness, taking in her painful admission. "This is no dream. It's for real, Laura. I've learned my lesson. I can have everything taken away from me: my career, my company, my money. But you know what? The two things I can't live without are you and the children. I'm nothing without you, Little Swan." Morgan caressed her cheek and held her luminous gaze, which radiated with a love for him he really didn't feel he deserved.

"I'm the luckiest man in the world, and I didn't know it, Laura. I took advantage of you and the family. I got in over my head, and I went to extremes—and you and the kids paid the price for me. God, what an awful price it was, too. . . ."

Laura closed her eyes, content to be held and protected by Morgan. She knew without saying it, that the work that still lay ahead of them was not going to be easy. She wasn't going to try to fool herself or lie to herself ever again. Too much that was important to her was at stake, and she was willing to make the commitment to work through any amount of pain in order to have a better, more complete life with Morgan and her children.

Easing away from him, she reached out and caressed his scarred face. "What about me not being able to have more children?"

Morgan felt tears fill his eyes as he studied her softly shadowed face and saw the grief there. With his thumb, he gently caressed her cheek. "It doesn't matter," he said thickly. "We're lucky to have a son and daughter, and that's enough for me, Little Swan."

"But...you wanted at least four children. So did I...."

Helplessly, Morgan shrugged. "If that becomes important to us again, Laura, we can always adopt, can't we?" Making a sound of frustration, he sat up and framed her face with his hands. "Listen to me, will you? I love *you*. I need you. I don't need you because you can have my children, all right? I didn't marry you or fall in love with you because you could have children, Laura. That happened to be a nice by-product of what we shared, and I'm thankful for our family, but I'm content with two children. We love them with our lives, and I'm the luckiest bastard in the world right now, Laura. I've got you, Jason and Katherine. I'm more than fulfilled. I've got it all."

Laura believed him. She felt the truth of his words to the depths of her soul. Sliding her hands across his, she managed a tremulous smile. "I like the two we have, too, darling. And no, I don't need four children. I just thought you wanted them...."

"Partly because I didn't talk clearly with you about it," he growled unhappily. "But you see? Talking is already removing some of the barriers between us, Laura. So maybe now things don't seem as bad to you as they once did? We have the two best kids in the world already, as far as I'm concerned."

Smiling, she nodded. "I believe you. I really do."

Relieved, Morgan grinned. "Good. What do you say we go to bed? I don't know about you, but I'm beat to hell. This is one day I'm glad is behind us. All I want to do," he said thickly as he caressed her hair, "is to lie in that narrow bed with you in my arms. What do you say, Little Swan? Does that sound good to you, too?"

Did it ever. Smiling tenderly, Laura allowed him to help her rise to her bare feet. She relaxed in his arms, a contentment she never thought possible filling her as he held her in a tight embrace.

"I love you, Morgan," she murmured.

Seeking and finding her lips, he kissed her hotly, letting her know just how fiercely he loved her in return. This time, Laura responded in kind, and he felt the strength of her mouth, the fire of her as a woman. Tearing his mouth from hers, his breathing ragged and his heart pounding like a sledgehammer in his chest, he rasped against her ear, "And I'll love you forever, Laura."

Chapter Thirteen

The next morning, Laura awoke to the sound of the cabin door opening and closing several times. She lay alone in their bed, hearing Mike Houston's low voice, then Morgan's responding. Their footsteps echoed hollowly on the pine floor, and she wondered why there was so much activity. Sitting up, she was shocked to see it was nearly eleven o'clock. She'd overslept!

As she hurriedly got out of bed and donned her robe, she heard the door close once more. Quiet descended on the cabin again. As she opened the door to the living room, she saw Morgan carrying something to the kitchen in his arms. Peripherally aware of the fragrant smells of coffee perking and bacon frying, she realized she actually felt hungry as she followed Morgan into the kitchen. He was busy cooking, and a huge

pile of magazines was stacked on the table near her
waiting plate. Standing in the doorway, she saw him
turn in surprise.

"You're up."

She smiled a little drowsily and pushed several
strands of hair off her brow. "Finally."

Morgan came over and slid his arms around her,
pulling her gently against him. He kissed her silken
hair and her temple, then inhaled her womanly fragrance. "Mmm, you not only smell good, but I wonder how you taste?"

Laura smiled beneath his lips as they came to rest
against hers. The gentle strength of Morgan's mouth
was more healing than he could ever realize. She kissed
him back, sliding her arms around his neck. As they
eased out of the kiss, she smiled up into his smoky
gray eyes, which burned with obvious desire for her.

"What was all that noise about? I know I heard
Mike's voice. Is something wrong?"

Morgan led her to the kitchen table and sat her
down where he'd laid out a sunflower place mat, a
plate and flatware earlier. "No," he replied as he returned to the stove, "it was just an idea whose time
was way overdue." He quickly scooped scrambled
eggs and bacon from two different skillets and placed
them on her plate. Popping two slices of bread into the
toaster, he gave her a triumphant smile.

Laura began to eat, surprised to find she felt rav-
enous. Morgan had that devilish look glinting in his
eyes, and she knew he was up to something. He came
and sat next to her, his elbows propped on the table.
"What idea?" she asked suspiciously.

He pointed to the huge stack of magazines. "I had Mike go into Sedona and buy a lot of different magazines this morning and bring them out for us." He frowned, suddenly serious, and held her gaze. "I remember when we were first married and you told me how you'd been adopted by your Marine Corps father and mother. You told me he'd been born in the Colorado Rockies and that you'd always wanted to live there someday. You told me how, as a child, you bought a scrapbook with your allowance and called it your 'Book of Dreams.' You would cut out pictures from magazines and paste them in the scrapbook— pictures of the mountains and log cabins, in hopes of someday making your dreams come true."

Laura sipped the coffee. She set it down and smiled softly. "Yes, I remember telling you about my 'Book of Dreams.'"

"You put all kinds of things into that scrapbook over the years."

Laughing lightly, Laura nodded. "I certainly did. I don't know how many times I toted it out and sat with my mother or father, talking over what my future husband would look like, how many kids we'd have and what they'd look like or where we were going to live." With a shake of her head, she murmured, "I wonder if they ever got tired of me going over and over those things I'd pasted in that scrapbook."

"I doubt it, Little Swan." Morgan reached out and captured her hand briefly. "And neither will I. Because that's what we're going to do for the next few days. You're going to create a new 'Book of Dreams' and tell me about everything you put in it." Triumphantly, he set a bottle of glue and a pair of scissors in front of her plate. "After you're done eating and have had a chance to shower and dress, you and I are going to sit here and do it. Together."

Tears flooded Laura's eyes as she looked at the raw hope on Morgan's face, heard his voice waver with deep feeling. "Oh, Morgan, that's such a beautiful idea...."

"It's more than that," he told her gruffly, squeezing her hand a little more tightly. "It's going to be my SOP—standard operating procedures—with you. It's time your dreams got explored, don't you think?"

Shaken, Laura was momentarily unable to speak. Her life had always centered around making Morgan and the children happy, not herself. But all that seemed to be changing—radically and suddenly. "Well," she stuttered, "but—but what are you going to do with whatever dreams I might put into this scrapbook?"

Morgan's smile was very confident and filled with love as he said, "I'm going to make them come true."

At the end of three days, Laura's new "Book of Dreams" was completed to her satisfaction. As she and Morgan sat at the kitchen table, the radio playing softly in the background, she watched him for a reaction. He'd said very little during the past days, except to occasionally nod his head or make sure she had more magazines if she needed them. Now, as they sat down in the late afternoon, coffee in hand, to discuss what she'd cut out, she felt an unbidden excitement.

"Okay, let's take a look at the final product," he murmured as he pulled the scrapbook to him. Opening it, he studied the first page. On it was a huge, beautiful, cedar-log home. Laura had also found some pine trees from another magazine and glued them in around it.

"There's more to this landscape," she said tentatively. "I just ran out of room on the first page."

He smiled a little and turned the page. On the second spread was a huge vegetable path and next to it, a wildflower garden. On the third page, he saw the rugged Rocky Mountains as a backdrop to two children playing happily by a stream, surrounded by tall rushes and wildflowers. On the next page two people, a man and woman, stood arm-in-arm on a grassy knoll watching a peach-colored sunset.

Laura sat very still, her hands clasped tightly in her lap, watching every emotion register clearly on Morgan's battered face as he slowly leafed through page after page. She could literally feel him digesting the dreams she'd cut out and pasted on those pages. Why was she so nervous? So afraid? Deep down, she had come to realize that Morgan was right: after seven years of living for him and their children, she'd never really learned to live for herself. In the wake of their latest revelations, Laura had realized more each day how much she needed time and creative expression to live out her life according to her own inner, spiritual needs. Morgan had told her repeatedly that the balance of power had shifted in their marriage—to her. But how was he going to accomplish that, beyond selling Perseus?

"All right," he said gruffly, "I think I've got a fair idea of what you need." He looked up and studied her shadowed blue gaze, seeing the tension around her mouth. He knew Laura was still wary of his promises to change, and he didn't blame her. "Rachel was telling me of a woman architect who lives here, in Oak Creek. She's world famous for the homes she designs. What do you say we make an appointment to see her and discuss the building of this cedar home for us?"

Laura's mouth fell open and she gaped at him. "But... where?"

Giving a lazy shrug, Morgan let a sliver of a grin leak through his serious demeanor. Taking her hand and holding it in his, he said, "What you didn't know is that I've been in touch with Wolf Harding. You know he owns Blue Mountain up in Philipsburg, Montana. Sarah, his wife, mines sapphires, and they live on one side of it." His grip tightened. "Wolf and Sarah are willing to sell us half of Blue Mountain, so we can build that Rocky Mountain dream home of yours. What do you think of that?"

Again, Laura was rocked by Morgan's decisions. She could only stare, but her heart was racing with joy. His gray eyes looked so grave, but she saw the glint in them, too, that proved he meant what he was saying. "Oh..." she whispered, touching her throat with her fingertips.

"*Oh?* As in, oh, that's a great idea? Or, oh, Morgan, that's a terrible idea?"

Laura felt the sunlight of his smile radiating upon her, and she offered him a full-wattage grin in return.

"It's a wonderful idea, Morgan! You really bought a mountain in Montana?"

"Yes." At the incredible pleasure in Laura's eyes, Morgan's heart expanded like a flower opening. Never had he felt as good as he did right now. The new life in Laura's eyes was something to behold, and the hope clearly written there rocked him as little else could. Finally, he was beginning to grasp just how much of her life had been given to him at the expense of herself. But now that they were truly becoming equal partners in the relationship, Morgan found it far more satisfying than what they'd shared before.

"Oh," Laura whispered, tears filling her eyes. "A real mountain."

"Yup, just like the one in here." And he opened to the page in her "Book of Dreams" that pictured a white-topped mountain swathed in the green of fir trees. "Wolf and Sarah understood what we needed. They didn't have to sell us the other half of their mountain, but they did."

"But Sarah makes their living off the sapphires. Won't we be taking away half their ability to make money by buying half their property?"

Morgan shook his head. "No. What you don't know is that Sarah just found an incredible deposit of cornflower blue sapphires—the biggest one is some fifty carats—and basically, they're set for life with this find."

"Wonderful!" Laura whispered, meaning it. She knew how hard Wolf and Sarah had struggled to make ends meet—Wolf working as a forest ranger and Sarah continuing her sapphire mining, faceting her finds and selling them to jewelry distributors. "They really deserve this kind of a break."

"Yes," Morgan agreed, "they do. Now maybe they can focus on other important things in their marriage."

"I know they both wanted children," Laura said. She rallied gamely, though reminded that she could never have them again herself. "They deserve every happiness."

Leaning over, Morgan kissed the back of her hand. "No question about that. So, how do think you'll like your new home, Mrs. Trayhern? Will a Philipsburg, Montana, address help fulfill your dreams?"

Her lower lip quivered. "Yes," she whispered, "it's a dream come true, Morgan. I just don't believe it. I never thought—"

"Good," he rumbled, satisfied. "Let me call this woman architect. We've got some designing to do. If we're lucky, we'll get things set in motion. In a couple of days, we can fly to the Cascades and set up temporary housekeeping at Jake's cabin. Then we'll have the kids flown out to be with us."

Laura nodded, overwhelmed. Finally, she managed to say in a broken whisper, "We'll be a family again...."

Morgan lay in bed with Laura in his arms. It was barely dawn at Jake's cabin in the pristine wilderness of the Cascade Range of central Oregon. Laura's warmth felt damn good to him. How he looked forward each night to sharing this bed with her. Had three months fled by already? He keyed his hearing to the room next door, where the children were sleeping soundly. Jason would wake up around seven, he knew, and little Katherine would follow shortly. Then the day's chaotic but fulfilling events would begin. But right now, it was only five-thirty, plenty of time to savor the silence—and Laura.

A sweet longing filled Morgan, as it always did when he awoke at this time of morning. In some ways the past three months had been like a visit to hell, in other ways, heaven. The children had finally settled in, and Morgan was amazed at their resiliency, considering the toll that had been taken. Even more profound was the fact that Jason, who'd been showing hyperactive symptoms, was calming down, and it was now that Morgan honestly began to see the cost to his family. Jason was reacting to the stress Morgan had always brought home with him from Perseus. The little boy picked up on his worries like all-terrain radar.

Little Katherine, who'd been still being breast-fed at the time of the kidnapping, was sleeping much better, too. She had been through nights where she'd wake up screaming—for no reason. Here at the cabin, Katherine was finally sleeping soundly through the nights, and Morgan knew Laura was especially grateful, since she was usually the one to get up and go to her.

Chickadees began chirping outside the window, and somewhere, far off, the high, warning shriek of a blue jay could be heard. Morgan thought it was probably reacting to the old cougar that lived about ten miles from the cabin, high in the cliffs where there was a cave. He and Laura hadn't been able to do much hiking yet, because of the weather, but with winter's hold on the mountains finally breaking, spring flowers were beginning to dot the surrounding landscape.

Laura... A pain filled him, along with a fear. They still hadn't been able to make love—because of the damnable rapes. Morgan found himself hating Garcia more every day. Dr. Parsons had warned him about Laura's on-again, off-again ability to be touched, kissed, held or loved. With the children underfoot, the possibility of lovemaking had become strictly a night-time affair, and Laura was still recovering from the trauma, desperately needing all the sleep she could get.

Morgan tried to take on some of the mothering role so Laura didn't have the pressure of caring for the children twenty-four hours a day. He was learning in no uncertain terms that being a housewife was a damned demanding and drudgery-filled job—and his admiration for Laura had increased tenfold as a result. His taking over half the family duties had brought them all much closer together as a unit, too, in a way that wouldn't have happened if he hadn't sold his business. In a perverse way, Morgan liked the change. He'd never realized the extent of the toll on him, until he'd gotten far away from the intense demands of Perseus.

Laura moved in his arms, her brow resting against his jaw. Her breathing was soft and shallow, and he could feel her stirring from sleep. Moving his hand along her slender arm, he felt the softness of her skin, the curve of her body fitting against his. The silk of her hair tickled his lips, and he smiled lazily as she pressed her full length against him like a cat stretching languidly. A part of him was scared to death of her rejection—once again—should he try to love her. But Ann had said to remain intimate with Laura on as deep a level as she could tolerate.

That was the frustration, he thought, as he eased Laura onto her back, his arm beneath her neck and cradling her shoulders. Neither he nor Laura knew when her rape trauma would rear its ugly head. Sometimes it was when he was kissing her. Other times, when he caressed her breast. Or, if he became too aggressive, she would instantly freeze and push him away. The worst was the look of terror in her eyes. It made Morgan feel like a bastard, and his emotions would flash to an overriding anger—toward Garcia. It was as if the drug kingpin was here, standing between them at their most intimate times together, and Morgan could taste his hatred for the evil man and what he'd done to Laura.

So he'd learned to go slow and easy, which wasn't all that hard for him. Morgan missed those times of passionate spontaneity he'd once shared with Laura. But if he grieved silently for that aspect of their old relationship, he never told her, because he didn't want to hurt or worry her.

Still, Morgan had seen progress in the intimacy they'd gradually established. The first month he'd learned not to play the rejected husband. Laura could no more help her flashbacks, or that out-of-body sensation that sometimes drove a wedge between them, than he could his occasional nightmares where he relived the horrors of that Vietnam hill. He watched now as Laura sleepily lifted her lashes to reveal smoky blue eyes. Smiling, he leaned over and caressed her parted lips. She tasted sweet and soft beneath his exploration, and he felt her moan, her arms sliding around his shoulders in invitation.

Her lips parted even more, and, feeling her hips move against his hardness, he groaned. Her silky hair swirled across her shoulder as he lifted the thick strands, easing his fingers across the top of her head in a gentle, kneading motion. Nothing relaxed her more than his combing her hair or gently massaging her scalp, he'd discovered. Another part of him waited with bated breath to be shoved away, or to feel her stiffen awkwardly in his arms—her nonverbal request, asking him to stop. How he wanted to love her completely! The ache in his loins burned through him as he allowed his hand to range tentatively down her arm to her waist.

Her skin was soft and giving as he cupped her hip and brought her against him. It was then that he felt her stiffen. It was nothing obvious, but mentally he cursed, placing a tight rein on his own raging needs. As he eased his mouth from hers, he opened his eyes and looked into hers. They were wide again—with fear. Damn it, anyway!

"Morgan," Laura began softly, "I'm—"

"Don't say it," he exclaimed harshly, easing away from her and sitting up. "You don't have to apologize, Laura." And she didn't. It wasn't her fault. He saw her crestfallen look, disappointment joining the guilt in her expression. He couldn't be impatient or angry under these circumstances, and he didn't want her to think he was upset with her. "Come here," he murmured, pulling her gently against him.

She came without a word, resting against his naked form, her head against his shoulder, her arm around his waist.

"That's better," Morgan murmured against her hair. He pressed a kiss to it and held her a little tighter for a moment.

"It was so wonderful, like before," Laura said in a whisper. "And when you touched my hip, I had this awful flashback, Morgan." She squeezed her eyes shut and pressed her cheek against his warm, strong shoulder. Biting back the words of apology, knowing they would only upset Morgan, she concentrated instead on the sensation of his hand moving slowly up and down the curve of her arm. The massive pounding of his heart told her how badly he wanted her. And she wanted him, too! At least, her heart did, though her mind seemed to control everything—including the flashbacks that came between them, chilling her ardor, preventing her from loving him physically.

"Listen," Morgan said gruffly, "I'm beginning to realize that rape is like war. They're one and the same." He caressed her slender jaw and looked deeply into her worried eyes. "You remember how many times when we were making love I'd have a PTSD flashback to Vietnam?"

"Yes," Laura said with a grimace.

"And how those flashbacks interrupted our lovemaking?"

"You're right, they did. I hadn't thought about it."

"Because," Morgan said gently, "over the years the flashbacks diminished, intruding less and less on us."

Laura felt hope spring up in her breast. "Yes, that's right, they did."

"So," he whispered, caressing her hair and placing a kiss on her brow, "this is no different. You didn't get angry with me for my flashback."

"No, but you felt bad about it coming between us."

"Yes," he admitted heavily, "I did. You went unfulfilled."

"So did you," she noted wryly, content to be held by him forever. Did Morgan realize how strong he was for her? It was more than just his physical size and strength—it was the strength of his heart, and his support of her.

The phone rang.

Morgan groaned and reluctantly released Laura. The phone didn't ring often, and when it did, he made a point to answer it, because it was usually Mike Houston with information they needed. Had they found that second hit man? He fervently hoped so as he shrugged on his terry-cloth robe and moved quickly into the living room to the phone.

Laura sat up in bed, ran her fingers through her mussed hair and decided she might as well get up, too. The mood had been spoiled anyway. She heard Morgan answer the phone tersely, followed by the usual grunts of "yes" or "no" that she'd heard so many times before. Retrieving her robe, she slipped it on over her silky pink nightgown and went to the bathroom.

She was filling the tub with water when Morgan entered the bathroom, an odd expression on his face as he shut the door behind him.

"Who was calling?" she asked, taking the jar of orange-scented crystals from the vanity.

"It was Mike."

Laura opened the jar and sprinkled a handful of crystals into the water. "What's up?"

Morgan leaned against the door, his hands in the pockets of his robe as he watched her. "Good news."

"Oh?" She set the jar back on the vanity and gathered up her hair with a pink ribbon so it would be off her neck.

"Yeah, the CIA just called Mike. Garcia was flying to Bogotá, Colombia, with thirty other powerful drug lords from around South America for a big meeting." He smiled a little. "The plane carrying them blew up in midair halfway to their destination." Morgan saw Laura's eyes go wide with shock, and she stood very still.

"Then—"

"He's dead. The whole lot of them are dead. There were no survivors, according to Colombian officials." Morgan snapped his fingers. "Just like that, all those bastards went up in a puff of smoke." His smile was savage and filled with satisfaction.

A chill went through Laura as she stood considering the news. "He's dead...." Garcia, her rapist, was dead. Somehow, the idea was liberating, and for a moment she felt guilty that she was glad he was no longer alive. It wasn't like her to wish anyone dead. Ever. At times, in sessions with Dr. Downey, she'd confided with great guilt that she'd like to kill Garcia herself for what he'd done to her. Laura hadn't felt good about admitting it, but Pallas had assured her it was a healthy, normal reaction.

Morgan moved over to Laura and pulled her into his arms. "You okay? You're a little pale."

She closed her eyes and sank willingly against him. His arms were strong and supportive, and right now, she needed that sensation. Slipping her own arms around him, she pressed her face against his robed chest. "I'm okay... just... in shock, I guess."

"It couldn't have happened to a nicer bunch," he growled, easing his fingers across her jaw. "Mike also said they caught the second hit man in New Orleans. He's in jail now, awaiting deportation."

"Thank God," Laura whispered, feeling even more weight falling from her shoulders. She hadn't realized until now how much tension she still carried in them. As if sensing her thoughts, Morgan began running his large hand slowly across her shoulders.

"We're free," he told her. "Really free, now. With all the major drug lords dead, the underlings will be scrambling to take over and rebuild their empires. They're going to be too busy in their own backyards to come after us again."

"You really think that, Morgan?"

"Yes, I do." He eased her away, dropping a quick kiss on her parted lips, and smiled down at her. "The CIA will take advantage of this shift of power. Mike said he's going to fly back down to Peru and help them create continued chaos in the drug industry—to try to stop it from re-forming, or at least from re-forming too quickly."

"But," she protested, "what about Ann? They're in love with each other! What will she do?"

"Mike said Ann's going down with him. She's submitting her resignation to the CIA and quitting Perseus." He smiled a little. "Mike's head over heels in love with her, and they're going to set up housekeeping in Lima, Peru. He'll be working with the Peruvian government at the capital, and Ann's going to start working with the city's poor, because doctors are always needed there."

"Will they be in danger, though?"

"Some," Morgan admitted, gently tracing the outline of one of her arched eyebrows. "They know the risks, Little Swan. They'll take steps to protect themselves."

"I'm so happy for them," she murmured. "Ann deserves someone like Mike. He's a neat guy—" she looked up at him, smiling "—like you."

Morgan cherished her lips, and felt her returning ardor as he absorbed her feminine form against him. The air was moist and filled with the fragrance of orange blossoms. "There's just something about us old, battered warriors, eh?" he teased as she moved from his embrace to shut off the water in the tub.

Laura removed her robe and hung it on a hook. "Yes, there's something very sexy, dangerous and provocative about you warriors," she teased in return, meeting his very male smile. She saw the desire smoldering in his eyes as she eased the nightgown over her head.

"Come on," she entreated, stepping into the over-size tub. "Join me?"

Morgan groaned. "The water smells like perfume."

With a lilting laugh, Laura held out her hand. "Oh? Big, bad old warriors can't stand a little perfumed water every once in a while? Really, Morgan, being a man doesn't mean you can't smell good."

"There's a difference between man smells and woman smells," he muttered defiantly, shedding his robe. He saw the impish quality dancing in Laura's eyes as he gripped her outstretched hand.

"Who knows?" she said, baiting him. "Something good might happen when we take a bath together. It's a new experience—why not try it? I thought you warriors were always up for new adventures."

Stepping into the warm water, Morgan grinned. A decided difference had come into Laura after hearing the news about Garcia. Maybe, just maybe, it would help her continue to get well—to know that the person who had victimized her had gotten his just reward. The gold flecks were back in her eyes, and for that Morgan was grateful. It was the first time he'd seen those shining sunlit flecks in far too long.

As they lowered themselves into the steamy, scented water, Morgan held Laura's returning smile as she picked up the soap. Life was getting better—one day at a time, one hour at a time—just as Dr. Parsons had promised. Right now, their new home was being built by contractors on Blue Mountain in Montana. By June, they would be moved in. The future seemed suddenly brighter and happier than ever before to

Morgan, and a fierce love swept through him as Laura moved to his side and began to provocatively slide the lathered soap across his shoulders and chest. In that moment, he knew without doubt that his marriage was whole again, and there would be no other woman for him ever but Laura.

Epilogue

"Look, Morgan!" Laura called from where she crouched in her wildflower garden. "Come and look."

He stood on the sun deck of their Montana home, his hands deep in the pockets of his Levi's. Jason and Katherine were helping their mother weed the garden, which bloomed in colorful profusion on the eastern side of their new home. Laura's face shone with joy, her once-pale skin turned a golden tan from her many hours in the sun spent working not only on her huge, oval flower garden, but on an even bigger vegetable patch.

Where had the past fifteen months fled since the fateful day when he'd found her unconscious on that trail? Morgan hesitated a moment on the deck, simply enjoying the sight of his family busily working together on a project they all loved. Since that day at the Donovan Ranch, Morgan had never regretted a single one of the major, life-altering decisions he'd made. His love for Laura and his children and their safety was more important to him than anything else in the world.

The warmth of the wood railing felt good beneath his callused palms as he leaned over to watch his family. Jason, the very active seven-year-old that he now was, rushed up and down the rows, picking at a weed here and a weed there, unconcerned about being thorough. Meanwhile, Katherine worked at Laura's side as they eliminated every last little weed among the brilliant, blooming flowers.

The straw hat Laura wore to protect her face made her look like an old Victorian print, Morgan thought. She wore a loose, summery white blouse and baggy, light blue trousers that had seen better days. But it was the smile always hovering around her lips that sent his heart pounding and made his lower body tighten instantly every time. Katherine liked coveralls, bright-colored ones, especially, and her blond hair was in tiny braids, the red ribbons matching the flush on her cheeks. Yes, Katherine decidedly took after Laura, while Jason was the spitting image of himself.

Running his hand distractedly across the smooth cedar rail, Morgan sighed. Nothing had made him happier in his life than seeing Laura cry with absolute joy when he'd flown her to Montana, and then driven her and the children to Blue Mountain to see their newly designed home. Stately Douglas firs rose nearly a hundred feet high all around them, and they'd walked the pine-scented land for many days, planning the details for her gardens. It was there that the final miracle had occurred, and Morgan had seen the last of the depression and terror lift from Laura.

He continued to write operation manuals for the government based on the exploits of Perseus teams over the years. To his own surprise, impressed by the accuracy of the manuals, twenty-five other democratic countries had signed up to make use of his world-class knowledge, and the price he charged as a consultant was high. High enough to give Laura her dream home, put money away for their children's college education and never have to worry about their golden years again.

Because of Laura's background as a military and technical writer, she'd easily fallen into helping him almost daily on the writing and rewriting of the manuals. They'd become a good team in so many new and satisfying ways that he'd never even dreamed of before. No longer was he an absentee parent, either. He was home every day, sharing the child-raising duties and house-related chores with Laura.

Morgan straightened and rubbed his hands on his jeans. The laughter and joy drifting up from the garden made him smile. In fifteen months there had been such a positive change in all of them. Looking up at the fir trees that embraced the house from a distance, he inhaled the fresh air into his lungs.

They were safe now. No longer would a drug cartel come after them. As a matter of fact, it had been Culver Lachlan, the Peruvian government and Major Mike Houston who had combined resources to eradicate the scrambling drug underlings to such a degree that their iron-fisted hold on Peru had been destroyed.

The other good news was that Mike Houston had married Ann Parsons a year ago. Now Ann was pregnant with their first child while she continued to work with Lima's poor in setting up free medical clinics. They were one happy couple, and Morgan wanted only the best for them.

With a shake of his head, he walked down the steps. His family was healing finally, and for the first time since his days in Vietnam, he was happier than he could ever recall. The sound of a car engine caught his attention and he looked up to see a blue Chevy Blazer driving slowly up their road. It was Wolf and Sarah Harding, come to take the children to Wolf's favorite swimming hole. Morgan lifted his hand in greeting as the couple pulled into the driveway. He'd never seen Wolf happier, either; Sarah was decidedly pregnant, and the homeopathic doctor from Philipsburg, Michaela, had told her she was going to have twins!

Morgan watched Laura stand when she saw Wolf and Sarah walking toward them. He felt warm inside as her smile blossomed. She raised her hand as the children raced to the gate, then past it toward their honorary "aunt" and "uncle." Having good friends on the other side of the mountain had helped all of them enormously, too, Morgan acknowledged.

Jason picked up a nearby knapsack packed with their swimming suits, towels and a lunch, and continued toward the Blazer. Katherine was a little more circumspect, running on her short, spindly legs, her hands opened wide. Sarah laughed and crouched down to hug the little girl while Jason got swept up by Wolf, who settled the boy on his shoulders.

It was a weekly tradition now, and Morgan was grateful to Wolf and Sarah. Without them playing baby-sitter, he and Laura would have been hard put to make the time they needed to sort out the deep, emotional problems created by Laura's rapes. Sarah had single-handedly come in and laid down the law to them very early on, telling them that under no circumstances were they going to heal properly without some quality time alone together.

So once a week, Wolf and she came and picked up the kids, planning a day with numerous activities such as swimming, hiking, going to Anaconda or in some way making healthy, educational fun for them. Jason and Katherine would stay overnight with the Hardings and return home the next afternoon.

It was good for the kids, too, Morgan realized as he continued to walk slowly toward Laura, at the gate blowing kisses to the children, who had already climbed into the Blazer, raring to go on their next adventure. Jason and Katherine were being taught independence from their parents at an early age, learning how to be flexible and get along with other people who loved and cared for them. And Wolf and Sarah got to practice their child-rearing skills. It was a plan that had worked well for everyone concerned.

As Morgan reached the gate where Laura stood, he saw her lift her chin. The straw hat shaded her face but didn't hide the flush across her cheeks. Her blond hair, although gathered in a ponytail, had escaped in tendrils that clung damply to her golden skin. The temperature was in the eighties today—hot for this part of the Rockies.

"I don't know who's more excited by these once-a-week adventures," Morgan said with a chuckle, watching Wolf back the Blazer out of the driveway.

Laura slid her arm around Morgan's waist. She smiled softly and leaned against his tall, proud frame. "Me, neither."

He removed her hat and kissed her brow. "Are you ready for your surprise?"

Her eyes shone as she turned in his arms. "I love these times," she said huskily, absorbing his male smile. "And I love you, too...."

Morgan leaned down and pressed a quick kiss to her mouth. He wanted more. So much more. "Come on," he rasped, "I've got everything packed. All I need is you."

Blue Mountain was more a dream manifested into reality than anything else, Morgan had decided a long time ago. They walked hand in hand down a deer trail that cut diagonally across the mountain. Laura had changed into a pale pink blouse and long navy rayon skirt dotted with tiny pink rosebuds. She wore sandals, since Morgan had told her the surprise wasn't far away and hiking boots wouldn't be necessary, though he carried a large pack on his shoulders.

Once a week, he planned these "surprises," all of them designed to get Laura and him away where they could be alone and intimate. Over the past year, the rape issue had remained between them like an insurmountable wall, but gradually, as Dr. Parsons had promised, with intensive therapy and Morgan's help and understanding, the wall had been dissolving. It hadn't been easy on either of them. Morgan hadn't realized the pervasive and murderous effects of the rape not only on Laura, but on him, as well. What had been taken from Laura had also been taken from him, and he'd had to deal with the rage and helplessness of that knowledge.

Now Laura looked forward to these times as much as he did. If they felt like making love, they would— to the extent that Laura's flashbacks would allow. Morgan had been taught that intimacy was more than just sex. It was about talking, caring and being sensitive to Laura's needs. It was about touching and holding, too. He'd had to work a lot on that angle of himself, and he was admittedly far better off with these new aspects of himself, because they allowed him to appreciate and enjoy Laura more fully than ever before.

"Okay," he said, tugging gently on her hand and drawing her to a halt, "we have to stop here, and I need to blindfold you."

Laura laughed gaily. "Oh, Morgan, I'll keep my eyes shut. I promise!"

He grinned and shook his head. "No way. Last week," he said, pulling a scarf from his pocket, "you said you wouldn't look and you did." He gestured for her to turn around. They stood on a small knoll, surrounded by firs.

Pouting playfully, Laura turned obediently, her laughter breathy and filled with excitement. "I tripped, Morgan! I had to open my eyes. It was a natural thing to do.''

Chuckling, he slipped the scarf across her eyes and knotted it carefully behind her head. "Well, there are no rocks on the path, so you can't use that excuse this time." He caught her small hand in his. "Come on, I'll help you." Unable to keep the excitement out of his voice, he guided her down the trail.

"You said I've never been where we're going?"

"That's right," he said, leading her carefully, watching the steep trail in front of him as it wound sharply downward. "Now, it's pretty steep here, Laura, so don't hurry." She was like an excited child, reminding him of Jason at the moment, barely able to contain her joy.

"Oh, Morgan!" She burst into laughter. "We aren't very far from our house. I must have been here!"

"No," he growled. "You think you know Blue Mountain, but this is one place I discovered when you and the kids were shopping in Anaconda for school clothes."

"Hmm," Laura whispered, taking small steps down the trail. "I hear water!"

"Ears like a wolf, eyes like an owl," he teased. At the bottom of the path, he eased around her and whispered, "All right, I'm going to take the scarf off. Are you ready?"

"Oh, hurry, Morgan! I can hear water, and to tell the truth, I need a bath!"

"Now—" he grinned "—I wouldn't say that." He unknotted the scarf, enjoying touching the thick tendrils of her blond hair in the process.

"You need one, too," she reminded him archly, shifting from foot to foot.

"Thanks," he retorted, laughing fully as he removed the blindfold.

Laura's eyes widened enormously and her hands flew to her lips. "Oh!" A small stream meandered around the base of Blue Mountain, and in one spot it widened to create the perfect swimming hole, with a meadow filled with wildflowers on the opposite bank. The meadow was small by Montana standards, but to Laura it was like a fairy-tale painting from a children's book, nearly knee-deep with grass and colorful blossoms.

"It's so beautiful," she exclaimed as she turned and looked up at Morgan. She saw the pleased look in his eyes and felt herself respond effortlessly to his powerful masculine presence. He stood with his hands draped casually on his narrow hips, a proud smile playing at the corners of his mouth.

"It's like you, Little Swan," he whispered, taking her into his arms and pressing her against him. She relaxed instantly, her head resting on his shoulder as he enclosed her in his arms.

"I feel like this meadow," she confided, her voice quavering with emotion. "I feel abundant, blossoming...." She twisted to look up at him. "I suppose you're going to say something like, yes, you are a blooming idiot."

Chuckling, he pressed a kiss to her temple. "You hurt my feelings, Little Swan."

"I saw that teasing look in your eyes," she said, elbowing him gently in the ribs. "Don't forget, I can almost read your mind at times, Morgan Trayhern. Eight and a half years of marriage gives me that ability."

Morgan couldn't argue. He was always amazed at Laura's intuitive ability, not only with him, but with their children as well. Grinning, he nipped her earlobe. She dodged away, laughing, but he kept her captive within his embrace.

Turning around in his arms, Laura smiled up at him as she slid her arms around his neck. "Let's go for a swim! I'm so sweaty, and so are you."

Arching his eyebrows, he murmured, "I didn't bring any swimming suits."

Hitting him playfully in the shoulder, Laura said, "Of course you wouldn't. You men are all alike."

Pretending hurt, he released her. Laura found a nice grassy place a few feet away from him and began to undress. "I can't remember everything," he said, unbuttoning his shirt, his gaze never leaving her. Everything Laura did was graceful. He would never tire of watching her. Her blouse dropped away and he was pleased to see she wasn't wearing a bra beneath it. The skirt was next. In seconds she stood proudly naked before him, her eyes half-closed, a sultry, teasing smile on her lips.

"I may have forgotten the swimsuits," Morgan said, his voice husky as he dropped his shirt in the grass, "but I think you forgot a few things, too."

Laughing impishly, she raised her arms toward the dark, turquoise sky, languishing in the rays of the sun as it struck her naked skin. "Not that you mind," she said, pirouetting toward him like a ballerina. She en-

joyed watching Morgan undress. His old weight had
returned, his strength and vitality with it. It hurt her
every time she saw those awful scars across his back,
but even they were fading with time, for which she was
glad.

"Did you bring towels?" she taunted as he, too,
stood naked, a burning look in his eyes.

"Sure," he muttered, gesturing to the knapsack.
"Towels, a blanket to lie on, wine to drink—later, and
food. Besides you, what else is there?" His mouth
curved teasingly as he walked toward her. At that moment, Laura loosened her hair so that it flowed down
across her shoulders. Her hair was long now, much
longer than he'd ever seen it. The golden strands
curled provocatively around her breasts. Something
seemed different about her body, but he couldn't quite
place what it was. She had lovely breasts, the kind a
man could cup, hold and suckle. And even after two
children, her waist was small. One of his favorite
places to touch was Laura's slightly rounded abdomen. It had a pearlescent quality, and he loved to run
his large hand across it, spanning it, feeling the softness and reminding himself that she'd carried two
children made from the pure love between them.

"No, you don't!" Laura cried as she dodged his
outstretched hand. With a yell, she leapt into the clear
blue water.

Morgan watched her dive, her golden hair darken-
ing and flowing behind her like a ribbon. She came up
for air on the opposite bank. Slicking the water from
her face, she gestured for him to come in. Did she

know how beautiful she was? Morgan wondered as he dived in after her.

The water was icy cold, and it took his breath away. He met Laura on the other side, and she scooped up a handful of sand, then another, rubbing it against his shoulders, back and hips. He did the same for her. There was nothing like sand to clean the sweat and freshen the skin to a bright, pink hue.

Laura danced away from him as he tried to wash the front of her with the sand. She quickly did the chore herself. Her hair lay wet against her her head, wrapped like a thick scarf around her long, beautiful neck and breasts. He ached to have her, and he saw the desire in her dark blue eyes for him. But instead of chasing her, he was content to continue to bathe.

Climbing out, Laura went to the knapsack and drew out the red plaid blanket, spreading it out across the thick, deep grass near the bank. She lay down on her back, stretching her arms above her head, allowing the sun and breeze to dry the water from her body.

Laura felt Morgan come to her side. A few drops of water splashed across her, and she lifted her lashes. Smiling, because he was sitting facing her, his arm across her body so she couldn't escape, she saw that he was going to kiss her and her lower body ached with need of him as she relished the sensation as never before. The rape had taken so much from her, and only in the past three months had she felt the return of her old sensual, sexual self. It had been wonderful discovering that it hadn't been entirely taken from her forever.

As Laura reached up, sliding her damp arms around Morgan's wet shoulders, gleaming in the sunlight, she felt as if she was drowning in the burning dark gray of his eyes. Automatically, her lashes swept downward, and she stretched forward to meet Morgan's mouth. She wasn't disappointed as she felt his arms go around her, sweeping her against him, their bodies meeting and melding slickly against each other.

The warmth of the sunlight and the cooling dance of air across Laura's sensitized skin combined with her dizzied senses as Morgan's mouth settled commandingly on hers. She tasted the sunlight on his lips, inhaled the pine scent that encircled him, mingling with the clean, male fragrance that was distinctively his. Easing her fingers through his wet hair, she opened her mouth farther, inviting him in, her breathing ragged and her heart pulsing with need.

As he kissed her more deeply, she felt Morgan's hand range downward to cup her breast. Molten heat sizzled through her, and she arched against him, a moan vibrating softly in her throat. He tore his mouth from hers, and she waited those exquisite seconds before his lips settled over the hardened peak begging for his attention. Fire seemed to jolt from her breast down to her very core. Helplessly, she arched within his arms and felt herself being placed on the blanket.

Sliding her fingers down across his massive chest, following the hard curve of his narrow hips, she wrapped her fingers provocatively around him. Instantly, he groaned, stiffening against her, his eyes snapping open, their dark, stormy look making her sigh with joy. At that moment, he was more animal than man, and she thrilled to his masculine strength covering her body, taking her, his hand moving her thighs apart to receive him.

The water provided a slick lubricant between them, and the heat of the sunlight combined with the heat they were generating made her feel as if they were fusing like hot metal. She threw back her head, a small cry escaping as she felt Morgan ease his hand between her straining thighs. A new, molten warmth flowed from her, and she felt his fingers move provocatively within the confines of her womanhood. Each movement made her arch harder and sigh with need for his touch. Her lashes swept closed, and she surrendered herself to him in every way. The fire of the sun, the chill of the water, the playful dance of the breeze all conspired to heighten her senses.

Somewhere in her spinning, delicious state, Laura felt Morgan slide between her thighs. How she'd waited for this exquisite moment! She felt his hands settle on her hips, lifting her slightly, and she arched willingly into those large, scarred hands. The moment she felt him sheath into her, a cry tore from her—a cry of utter pleasure combined with acknowledgment of their union, of their becoming one again.

No longer did Laura see their union as something to take for granted. No, the rapes had taught them differently. Now each time she was able to stay connected, in her body, and focus on the fact that it was Morgan touching her and loving her, she experienced a miracle.

Laura felt Morgan move powerfully within her, taking her, claiming her for his own. He was strong as

he surged into her, and she held him with all her
woman's strength and tenderness as he began to rock
her hips in a rhythm as ancient as the world that now
embraced them. She gave herself freely, fully to Morgan, matching his rhythm, pulling him even more
deeply into the confines of her sacred place, which
burned with molten fire. They moved in a unison born
of years of loving—and months of careful relearning.
Laura was forever amazed and grateful that each time
they loved was better than the last—more sacred in a
way that not only touched her heart, but grazed her
very soul. At eighteen, she hadn't known lovemaking
could have this deeply spiritual aspect, but now, as a
mature woman, she knew and appreciated this new
awareness—this new level of exquisite pleasure.

An explosion of heat rushed through her lower
body, and Laura felt Morgan stiffen in almost the
same instant. She felt a wonderful joy in climaxing
together, at the same moment, for it didn't always
happen that way. She wrapped her legs around his,
heightening his pleasure, even as she relished his powerful arms around her, holding her so tightly that her
skin seemed to dissolve and become his. Intense waves
of pleasure washed over her, and she sighed, clinging
to him and reveling in the golden moment they shared.

Little by little, Laura became aware of the sunlight
warming her once more, the breeze dancing over them
as they lay on the blanket, on their sides, still holding
each other. The gurgle of the creek entered her consciousness, and slowly she opened her eyes. Morgan
was slightly above her, propped on his elbow, study-

ing her in the silence. His gray eyes were half-closed, thoughtful, still banked with coals of desire. She smiled tenderly and turned onto her back, content just to be close to him. Reaching up, she threaded her fingers through his drying hair. Despite the horrors and hardships Morgan had endured in his forty-some years of living, he looked stronger and more handsome to her now than ever before.

And Laura knew it was because of the decisions he had made fifteen months ago. No one was more grateful than she for his unselfish choices. It had taken that kind of dramatic change and commitment from him to help her overcome the rapes. Without that, she wondered if she would have healed as well as she now had.

"I love you," she quavered, sliding her fingers across his scarred cheek.

Morgan leaned down and cherished her smiling lips. "And I love you with my life, Little Swan," he rasped, sliding his hand down her ribs to rest on her hip.

Laura reached up, framing his face with her hands, mere inches separating them. "I have a wonderful surprise for you, Morgan."

He frowned at the undisguised, raw emotion in her voice, then smiled a little. "What is it?"

Laura smiled tenderly and took his hand, placing it against her belly. "Haven't you noticed something different about me?"

Morgan frowned again. His eyes widened. He gave Laura a shaken look, then stared down at his darkly suntanned hand spanning her abdomen and back into her radiant blue eyes. *"You're pregnant?"* The words came out in an explosion of disbelief. The gynecologist in Fairfax, Virginia, had told Morgan in no uncertain terms that Laura would never conceive again.

Laura laughed softly and sat up, throwing her arms around his neck and burying her face against his neck. "Oh, Morgan, I'm three months along! That first time we were able to truly make love, I conceived! It's been killing me to wait until today to tell you!" She laughed freely and kissed him repeatedly all over his face like a happy puppy.

"But," Morgan growled, gripping her by the arms, staring at her flushed features, "the doctor said—"

"What do doctors know?" She laughed, throwing her arms around his neck. "Morgan, I'm pregnant! Isn't it wonderful? Michaela said the pregnancy is fine. I'm fine!"

Stunned, Morgan continued staring at her. One of the things Laura had done shortly after moving to Philipsburg was to visit Dr. Michaela, the homeopathic physician who served the small community. Sarah had gone to her for help from time to time, and their smoke-jumper friend, Pepper Sinclair-Woodward, swore by Michaela's magic with alternative medicine.

"B-but—" he stammered, "how? I—I don't understand."

Trying to contain her joy, Laura knelt in front of him, her hands on his shoulders. "First of all, are you happy about it, darling?"

"Well...of course I am," he rasped, sliding his hand along her jaw and drowning in the joy in her eyes. "But I'm worried, too."

Laura shrugged. "I went to Michaela for a homeopathic constitutional treatment right after we moved here, Morgan. You remember that."

"Yes. Sarah said it might help you with the emotional problems resulting from the rape."

"Exactly," Laura said, smiling. "And it did. Well, what I didn't know but learned from Michaela is that homeopathic treatments not only works on a person mentally and emotionally, but physically, too." She shook her head and reached out to take both his hands. "I didn't tell you about one conversation Michaela had with me quite a while back. She examined me as any other doctor would, and she said that with homeopathic treatment, there might be a chance I could have children again."

"This isn't making sense," Morgan muttered. "How could conventional medical treatment say one thing and this alternative method another?"

"Proof's in the pudding, isn't it?" she teased, laughing. "Michaela said that scar tissue sometimes could, with homeopathic treatment, be dissolved. I didn't believe it, either, Morgan, but over the months, it was happening. And at that point—" she sighed, brushing several strands of hair away from her eyes "—I really began to believe what Michaela was saying all along—that I could have children again. I didn't tell you because I didn't want to get your hopes up, Morgan. I didn't want us to fail at this. I kept it to myself and hoped it would work." Her hands tightened around his and she shrugged. "It did!"

Morgan shook his head, stunned. "I'll be damned."

"Are you happy?"

"Of course I am, Little Swan." He pulled her back into his arms and they sat looking out over the mirrorlike surface of the deep blue water. He kissed her cheek. "Does Michaela think you can carry this baby to term?" he asked, recalling the trouble they'd had with Katherine coming early.

"Yes, she does. You know, half her homeopathic practice is mommies-to-be, babies and children. Michaela has fifteen years of experience, and I trust what she knows, Morgan. She feels I can deliver our baby to term, healthy and without labor problems."

"Because of your homeopathic treatments?" he wondered aloud.

"Yes. But Michaela isn't going to take any chances. I see her monthly for examinations and checkups. She gives me different remedies." Laura eased her head to the left and looked up at him. "I didn't even have morning sickness this time, Morgan, because she gave me a remedy that stopped it. Isn't that wonderful?"

Amazed, Morgan nodded. Gently, he covered her abdomen with his hands. "A baby," he whispered unsteadily.

"Our baby, rising out of the ashes of our love for each other," she reminded him softly. "She's like the fable about the phoenix—the bird that's destroyed by fire, burned to ashes and arises even more beautiful and strong into a new phoenix.

"Our love has gone through those fires, darling. We were both destroyed and reduced to ashes ourselves. We've risen out of that horrifying past—and look at us now! We're better and happier than before. Yes, this little girl is definitely our phoenix child, a gift for having the courage to fight back, to survive and put our love back together." Her voice trembled. "She is about our redefined, newly discovered love, Morgan. I've never felt happier or more at peace with myself, with you and our family than now. I have my hope back, and life looks like such a rich, unfolding adventure to me now—thanks to you helping me survive and climb back on my feet. . . ."

Morgan saw the tears in Laura's eyes and knew he had matching tears in his. Running his hands gently over her swelling abdomen, he felt too emotional to speak. Laura sighed softly, leaning back against him. The pond, the green grass and bright flowers blurred before his eyes. "I had my dreams torn from me so many times in the past," he whispered raggedly against her ear, "that eventually I quit dreaming. Then you walked into my life like a lightning bolt out of the blue, and my whole life was upended—in a positive way."

He pressed small kisses along Laura's neck and jaw, feeling her quiver with joy. His heart felt as if it would explode with the intense happiness he was experiencing. No one deserved the joy he felt, Morgan thought. Especially not him. Yet somehow the universe had given him a third chance. And he was taking it, come hell or high water. With Laura and their children, he could do anything it took to survive. Anything.

"A Christmas baby, huh?" he rasped, smiling and enjoying the feel of her lounging against him.

"Yes—" Laura sighed "—a Christmas baby."

"We couldn't ask for a better gift, could we?"

"No," she whispered softly.

"A baby girl, eh?"

"Katherine Alyssa will have that sister she always wanted. And Jason will learn to be a big brother all over again."

Gently, Morgan turned Laura so that she lay in his arms, her face inches from his own as he probed her radiant blue gaze, his voice thick with raw emotion. "I love you, Little Swan. Forever and beyond eternity."

* * * * *

COMING NEXT MONTH

Take 4 bestselling love stories FREE

Plus get a FREE surprise gift!

Special Limited-time Offer

Mail to Silhouette Reader Service™

3010 Walden Avenue
P.O. Box 1867
Buffalo, N.Y. 14269-1867

YES! Please send me 4 free Silhouette Special Edition® novels and my free surprise gift. Then send me 6 brand-new novels every month, which I will receive months before they appear in bookstores. Bill me at the low price of $3.12 each plus 25¢ delivery and applicable sales tax, if any.* That's the complete price and a savings of over 10% off the cover prices—quite a bargain! I understand that accepting the books and gift places me under no obligation ever to buy any books. I can always return a shipment and cancel at any time. Even if I never buy another book from Silhouette, the 4 free books and the surprise gift are mine to keep forever.

235 BPA AW6Y

Name	(PLEASE PRINT)	
Address	Apt. No.	
City	State	Zip

This offer is limited to one order per household and not valid to present Silhouette Special Edition® subscribers. *Terms and prices are subject to change without notice. Sales tax applicable in N.Y.

USPED-995   ©1990 Harlequin Enterprises Limited

Bestselling author

RACHEL LEE

takes her Conard County series to new heights with

A CONARD COUNTY Reckoning

This March, Rachel Lee brings readers a brand-new, longer-length, out-of-series title featuring the characters from her successful Conard County miniseries.

Janet Tate and Abel Pierce have both been betrayed and carry deep, bitter memories. Brought together by great passion, they must learn to trust again.

"Conard County is a wonderful place to visit! Rachel Lee has crafted warm, enchanting stories. These are wonderful books to curl up with and read. I highly recommend them."
—*New York Times* bestselling author
Heather Graham Pozzessere

Available in March, wherever Silhouette books are sold.

HOW MUCH IS THAT
COUPLE IN THE WINDOW?
by Lori Herter

Book 1 of Lori's Million-Dollar Marriages miniseries
Yours Truly™—February

Salesclerk Jennifer Westgate's new job is to live in a department store display window for a week as the bride of a gorgeous groom. Here's what sidewalk shoppers have to say about them:

"Why is the window so steamy tonight? I can't see what they're doing!" —Henrietta, age 82

"That mousey bride is hardly Charles Derring's type. It's me who should be living in the window with him!" —Delphine, Charles's soon-to-be ex-girlfriend

"Jennifer never modeled pink silk teddies for me! This is an outrage!" —Peter, Jennifer's soon-to-be ex-boyfriend

"How much is that couple in the window?" —Timmy, age 9

HOW MUCH IS THAT COUPLE IN THE WINDOW? by Lori Herter—Book 1 of her Million-Dollar Marriages miniseries—available in February from

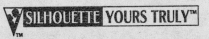

Love—when you least expect it!

You're About to Become a *Privileged Woman*

Reap the rewards of fabulous free gifts and benefits with proofs-of-purchase from Silhouette and Harlequin books

Pages & Privileges™

It's our way of thanking you for buying our books at your favorite retail stores.

PROOF OF PURCHASE
Offer expires October 31, 1996
SSE-PP98

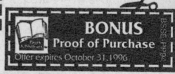

BONUS
Proof of Purchase
Offer expires October 31, 1996
BSSE-PP98

Harlequin and Silhouette— the most privileged readers in the world!

For more information about Harlequin and Silhouette's PAGES & PRIVILEGES program call the Pages & Privileges Benefits Desk: 1-503-794-2499

Silhouette®
™

SSE-PP98